I0679679

GREEN EMERALDS

AND

HEIST CLUB

BY
LINDA MCKOWN

Publisher LindaMcKownAuthor LLC

Scottsdale, AZ

1

Green Emeralds and Heist Club

ISBN-13: 978-1-7344095-0-5

Library of Congress Control Number: 2019920511

Author:
LindaMcKownAuthor LLC
11574 E Running Deer Trail
Scottsdale, AZ 85262
https://www.lindamckown.com

Any names of people and entities are fictitious in this story having been created by the author's imagination.

Front Cover Photo of the book was purchased from Shutterstock. Book title manipulation was done by Joseph McKown

Dedicated to my family, friends, and readers. This book is about second chances. Everyone deserves the opportunity to live their life to the fullest. Some of us know the second time around is way better.

Table of Contents

1 Casing the Casinos

Sandra Delray went to the Green Room gambling tables at the Splendor and Devon Casino in Las Vegas, Nevada. Her women's club would be at the hotel for four nights.

Sandra was playing poker in a long black stretch velvet dress. A good-looking man approached.

"Hi, gorgeous, do you mind if I sit next to you?"

Sandra looked at the man.

"This is a free country. I'll be leaving at the end of this hand."

The man scrutinized the woman.

"I've run into my second female this evening that has been super touchy. There must be a movement happening called hashtag no men. I think that I'm going to try the casino across the street. Their building gets the sun in the morning. Maybe I'll run into a woman with sunshine in her eyes instead of gloom and doom."

Sandra looked at her watch. Danielle was late. She wished her dress was not so tight and low cut. Her dress was a magnet for weird men. She was glad the man left their table. Surprised at her cards, she finished playing the game and won.

Another man approached. This one was tall, dark-haired, and very handsome.

"Great hand. You know how to play cards. I'm the manager of the casino, Craig Connor. If anyone bothers you again, please let me know."

Sandra didn't want to be noticed by management at this casino. Her group would be staying here in the future. She did need to respond. Her blue eyes looked into his hazel eyes.

"Hi, I'm Sandra Delray from Phoenix. My friends are late in their arrival. I thought that I could keep myself occupied by playing cards."

"Good. We're glad you have chosen our hotel and casino. You and your friends should have an excellent time."

He handed her six tickets to the evening's performance at his casino and five dollars off lunch at one of their restaurants. Sandra looked at the listed performers. The show was a comedy act.

She stood up and looked in his overly bright eyes inspecting her blonde hair. She never met the man before. The manager acted as if he knew her.

"Thank you very much. I see my friends are at the door."

Craig nodded to the game table boy who slid her chips to the edge and put them in a bag for her to take to the cashier when she was ready.

The manager watched her walk away and meet two other equally gorgeous women. They were redheads and appeared to be twins. He overheard her say Danielle and Dawn in her greeting. His casino was looking up with beautiful women arriving.

Sandra approached the two women. She was disappointed to see Danielle talking to the first man she saw at the poker table. The man saw her coming and left the casino. Sandra frowned at Danielle.

"What's wrong? He only wanted directions to the High Tower Plaza Hotel. The hotel was across the street. I pointed out how close he was to the building."

Dawn watched Sandra's expression. She needed to intervene.

"I know, but she's really good at other things like the electrical stuff. We can trust her to do the job. Also, Darcy will be arriving shortly to again review the plumbing requirements."

"Keep her away from that man. He scouts out women and is probably out of funds from gambling. We also have a slight problem."

8

She motioned for them to go to their rooms where they could talk without any cameras.

Once in their three adjoining rooms on the seventh floor, she told them about her encounter with the manager. Sandra ran her hand through her long hair after untying the back bun. She could think better without the black velvet hair constraint.

Dawn was envious of the woman's sleek hair. She commented, "I thought we were to play low key at this hotel. We can't have anyone become suspicious about our business."

"I know. Candy and Kim should be arriving later. We might as well eat dinner. I'm hungry."

The three women went to the lunch buffet dining hall and ate. After an hour the other three women joined them and filled their plates. They complained about their flight. There was a thunderstorm that delayed takeoff.

Craig was in the control room of the hotel viewing the screens of the tourists at his hotel. He saw the dining hall and the table of six women. He showed the group to his head security officer.

"I have a feeling about this group. Make sure you watch them."

His security officer, Kevin, looked at the women. He noticed Dawn.

"I like the woman in the camel coat with black leather boots. She looks classy."

"Kevin Meadow, we're not going to bother these women. You are also very married. We only need to watch them for one day. Then I'll determine if we need any further screening. The woman in black velvet should especially be watched. She seems to be in command."

Some of the women went to their rooms. Danielle and Sandra went back down to the main floor casino. They were looking for all the security cameras.

Using their cell phone to take selfies and a special compact holding a tiny camera, they captured all but two cameras.

Sandra stood talking with Danielle. She tapped her nose which was their sign to minimize their conversation to simple words.

"We're missing something. Oh, my earring is gone."

Danielle found the hoop earring in the fold of Sandra's top.

"Here let me put the earring back in. There now we have the two. I can see the lock on the earring is set."

Danielle used her eyes to show Sandra the location of two very tiny cameras. Sandra positioned herself to one side and took a selfie. She took a second selfie opening her mouth and licking her lips.

They walked ten feet and she handed her cell phone to Danielle.

"Let me do something sexy for Henri."

Sandra turned so her low-cut back was in the picture. She glanced over her shoulder with a wicked smile. There was a pumpkin seed in her mouth. Danielle started whistling a song. Sandra bent over laughing. Danielle took the shot.

"Perfect."

They went to their hotel room to review their photos.

Craig checked with the hotel's security control room. He looked at the special computer file. He watched the still shots of the two women.

"Damn, they found our tiny cameras. Will you look at Ms. Sandra Delray! She's mocking us. Is that a pumpkin seed?"

Kevin, his security man, looked at the still shots.

"She is a female Arabian all right. Do horses like pumpkin seeds?"

Craig looked at Kevin.

"Right, move along, Kevin. Your boss needs input. We are talking a professional is in the building. I haven't seen the likes of her and her keen ability to find our newly installed cameras. She is very, and I repeat, very good! I've been working here for seven years and never saw this type of move. We are so out of step in the cybercrime game."

"You're comparing her to my horse at my friend's ranch? My horse doesn't know she is a pro. This woman does. We don't have much cybercrime in Vegas. However, I'm sure she knows how to hack a computer."

"Yes, your horse is stunning and mischievous when the males are around. This woman knows she is top-notch. Look at the way she walks. Confidence to the maximum. I would say some modeling or other key experience happened besides computers. I would recognize her again on our screens. She is leading the other female Arabians. That is a dangerous situation."

"I agree. She and her friends are up to something. All of them may be involved in casing the casino. I don't think they are looking for wealthy men."

Kevin looked again at the sexy shots.

"I don't know if men are their game either. But they most definitely are going to be back. This first run is a check on our casino and the one across the street."

Craig shut down the computer file.

"Let's do a background check on Ms. Delray. Find out the rest of their activities while here. I've already given her six tickets to the comedy show and our standard discount coupons. When the full background check on her has arrived, I would like to review the document right away."

Craig Connor left Kevin. The next four days he reviewed the casino floor. Whenever he saw Sandra Delray, he was very cordial. He watched her when she wasn't looking.

Sandra watched Craig whenever she could avoid their security camera's range. She noticed he wore expensive suits with an expensive tie and white dress shirt. Mr. Connor was always impeccably well-groomed. She watched him socialize with his guests.

In the evening Craig went to his penthouse room on the top floor. He had a good idea of what the six ladies were up to in the next few weeks. He would need to make some decisions.

He would wait to see if the ladies returned. This trip to Vegas might be a checkoff. Vegas was on many people's bucket lists. He tried to tell himself his hotel was a perfect place for pleasure.

Craig wondered who the person was named Henri? The last selfie Ms. Delray took set his heart to beat faster. She was surprised by her friend and let down her guard. She dropped her mask. He saw a woman who enjoyed a good joke.

"You are good. Someone has taught you valuable skills. I'll bet there's a lot more underneath. Henri's possibly a boyfriend."

On the fourth day, Craig was with Kevin in the security room.

"Her background check is excellent. There are no red flags. She looks normal. She attended high school, college, and bought a new car, new condo, etc."

Kevin handed his boss the report. He continued with his verbal report.

"The first day the women checked into our casino. Sandra didn't go to the comedy performance. The second day, the women went shopping except Sandra went to the race car track. On the third day, the women went swimming and Sandra went skydiving. On the fourth day, they all went to the High Tower Plaza Hotel. Two of her group took cooking lessons, two went to the spa, one read in the lobby, and Sandra played cards."

"What about the evenings on days two through four?"

Kevin looked at his notes. "The women went out to eat. Sandra stayed in her hotel room."

Craig wondered why Sandra stayed in her room. People usually didn't stay in their rooms in this town.

"Fast cars and skydiving are her interests. Ms. Delray likes to live near the edge. She is not afraid."

"I'd say fearless is my guess."

Kevin continued his report. "Five of the women have checked out of the hotel. We are waiting for Ms. Delray."

Sandra looked around her hotel rooms. Without her friends, there was quiet. She packed her papers and soon would follow. She was leaving Mr. Craig Connor's elegant and expensive hotel.

Stopping by the lobby front door, she turned. Sandra felt brave and couldn't resist. Mr. Connor wasn't in control. She was.

Sandra looked directly at the security camera for a full minute before she smiled and left the hotel. She dared him to follow.

Craig was going to speak with her before she left when he saw on the screen a van pull beside the lobby door.

"The Australian band has arrived. I'll go down and greet them."

2 Visit with Fiona

Trust was important on this mission. The women's club met weekly and time was getting short. The other women would wait for Sandra's final signal. Afterward, they would all meet in Italy. An agreed-upon wait period for the media frenzy to die down would be required. The women selected a projected date in the future.

Sandra drank her iced tea and placed the glass on the kitchen table at Darcy's house in Phoenix. She was in town for two weeks.

"Oh, shit, I forgot about the insurance on the emeralds."

She rolled the idea around her brain. There was no plan surfacing for the moment. The heist soldering, moving any pipes, and construction out of the way was easy.

"Sometimes envelopes open due to lack of glue or heavy rain gets into the box. Fiona needs to make sure the insurance on her house is paid in case we need a backup. The other companies might dispute the loss location.

Sandra congratulated herself.

She looked at the clock. Tomorrow, her team would imitate the drill of entering the sewer, moving from one building to another and using a heat duct for entry into the hotel's boxes. There was a warehouse rental where they set up the scene for their rehearsal.

"The plan appears perfect. I need to make sure there are no mistakes. My women will clear the timed runs."

Sandra ran the drill in her head. Sewer maintenance costumes were ordered. She rechecked the names they used. The names on the other garments matched the company the two casinos used for plumbing problems."

Darcy was already hired as an assistant at the water heater firm. Next week Darcy would start work at the Johnson Water Heater firm in Las Vegas. She would get promoted once she received her plumber's license. The women believed she would be allowed to go on some of the work calls to the casinos beforehand.

Sandra stopped herself.

"I can halt this heist right now. I can break away. Maybe this job is a little overboard or plain crazy? What if my girls decide to dump the plan and impeach me? They could turn against me. People turn on you all the time. No, they wouldn't, Sandra.

They have nothing to lose except a boring life. Take Kim's advice and get a grip."

None of the other women called Sandra. This was the last day anyone could back out. Her phone was perfectly silent. The police didn't arrive to arrest her. The women in the heist club wanted to continue.

"The game is in my hands. We proceed forward. From now on, we move silent and fast. We move so fast that no one hears or sees us."

The clock read one o'clock in the morning. Sandra couldn't sleep.

"There has to be a better way."

She peered out the slot in the metal roller blinds and watched the stoplight on the corner. The light stayed green unless some activity caused the light to change. A car drove to the corner. The light changed red.

"A button or switch inside the case causes the change."

Sandra developed a flash of brilliance. She waited and watched the sun slowly rise. At nine o'clock, a friend was called.

The warehouse test run by the women would have to continue without her.

Sandra Delray was on an airplane to California. Driving the rental car, she knew the way to her friend's house. Stepping out

of the car, she walked to the front of the
house and punched the button on the
doorbell of a beautiful five-million-dollar
home in the Los Angeles hills. The lawn
was large and perfectly manicured by master
gardeners. The huge palm trees swayed with
the wind.

Jarret answered the door.

"Good day, Ms. Delray. This is very
nice. We were talking last night about how
much we would enjoy a visit. Mrs. Kendrell
is waiting for your arrival. She is in the pool
area. You know the way. Shortly, I'll bring
some refreshments and salads for your late
lunch."

"Thank you, Jarret. I do know my
way."

She walked through the large marble
entryway into the living room and through
the dining room past the table. A tea cart
stood in the corner near the hutch. She
opened the patio door and stepped outside.
The day was warm and perfect for
swimming.

Sandra saw the aging actress sitting
in a stuffed lounge area near the pool. The
pool area was cleaned that morning and
parts of the lawn were still wet.

The elderly woman wore gold
jewelry, a black full-length swimsuit, and a

black and white long lounge top. Her hair wore a black band to hold the hair up. Fiona obviously went swimming before she arrived.

"Hello, Fiona, how are you? Thank you for seeing me at the last minute. We need to talk. I see your roses are blooming. The smell is wonderful."

Fiona motioned for her nephew's ex-girlfriend to sit down.

"We have missed you. I'm so glad to see you, too. I was devastated when Demonte left you. He told me about a horrible woman, Peg-something-or-other. Then he found the nerve to marry the Peg-person and did the quick wedding without my approval. The woman doesn't even want children, but she wasn't smart on that score. I imagine her kitchen is a mess. Demonte smells of hamburger and onions when he comes over."

Sandra sat in the green lounge chair next to her friend.

"Her name is Petrissa, not Peg, and my understanding is that she is twenty-one years old. I'm embarrassed by the whole episode. I have moved on."

Fiona took a sip of the drink Jarret handed her.

"Petrissa is a child and looks at my house as if she's going to own it someday.

21

She has touched all my bronze statues and took pictures of them. Plus, she took snapshots of my paintings. She went into my bedroom. Jarret shooed her out. The little deer statue must be cleaned by Jarret constantly. She doesn't even try to hide her attempts from me. Demonte Duran is a bad boy. He is my dead sister's only child. We have been granted a reprieve. We haven't seen Demonte and Petrissa for some time. They are in South America traveling."

Sandra took a piece of the apple and brie cheese bites.

"These are so delicious," said Sandra.

The two women ate the various pieces of fruit and salad from the large platter. The older woman took her cloth napkin and daintily dabbed her mouth. She grabbed a tube of lipstick from her bag and smeared the coral color on her dried lips.

"Appearances are everything, you know, especially at my age. You never know who will come knocking on your door. Men pop up out of nowhere. Now, tell me the reason for your visit. I'm glad you have found some new women friends to help you get through the breakup mess and luckily remove yourself away from my nephew. Tell me about your ladies."

Sandra gave her a brief synopsis of her group and their various skills. She told her about one of their meetings. Fiona laughed along with her.

"Your women's club sounds like great fun. Do you allow elderly women in your club?"

Sandra took a leap of faith that their friendship would hold.

"I understand you have been invited by the Tiff Sander Jewelers to again showcase your emeralds in Las Vegas. I remember the other time you displayed your jewelry. I attended the show and subsequently, met Demonte."

"Yes, they have booked me in the High Tower Plaza Hotel. I'm hoping by showing the emeralds that I might find a buyer for the jewels. I've tried a private investor. The man was an absolute thief and would only give me a third of their net worth. I did get him to reach almost the halfway point of their net worth, but the amount still seemed too low."

Sandra was pleased. The man's name might be valuable in the future.

"The insurance company for the emeralds must have provided you with a new evaluation if you are going to show the jewels?"

Fiona withdrew the paperwork the insurance company gave her from the red, green, and blue striped beach bag and handed the papers to her visitor.

"Whew, thirty-five million is a lot of money. The clause covers theft on your property once the Tiff Sander Jeweler's agent, Mr. Sloan, arrives, completes his inspection, and deposits them in the case. The other insured place is at the show hotel."

Fiona nodded.

"Interesting. What about the security company transport?"

Fiona grabbed a lettuce-wrapped chicken salad piece and pulled the large toothpick out. She took a new cloth napkin.

"There's an addendum E for the transport company."

Sandra found the page and was satisfied.

"The papers look like you are all legally covered. You need Horatio to examine the papers and make sure your home insurance has been paid," said Sandra.

Fiona looked craftily at her guest.

"Tell me that you are still playing your violin. I was very upset when Demonte canceled your lessons. I wanted to pay for them. The lessons were my gift. He wouldn't budge and the other instructors were booked for the season. I couldn't get you back in."

Sandra wistfully remembered her violin sitting in the leather case at Darcy's house.

"A string is broken, and I need a break from my music. Eventually, I will get back to playing."

"Good. You are too talented to stop playing. Your instructor thought that you could conduct a whole orchestra if you wanted. He told me what I already knew; you are a very smart person and highly capable."

Sandra blushed but was pleased.

"Thank you. You have brightened my day."

Fiona was happy with her only friend.

"All my friends have died in this town. The crowd in the rose and garden clubs are younger. You are my only visitor at my home for some time. Even my hairdresser mysteriously passed away. She more than likely breathed in too many of those pneumonia and odd cleaning chemicals. The beauticians are responsible for killing the bugs that come into the shop."

Sandra looked at Fiona's long hair. The woman needed a good trim and gray or silver highlights.

"You mentioned an idea on the phone. I'm interested in getting the full price for my emeralds or a price that's reasonable. I want to move to Rome and live in the city. My friends are there, and I need this money to live out the rest of my life. I don't want to cut back on giving to my charities."

Sandra explained her thoughts about how they could manage their part of a combined business transaction.

The elderly actress stopped eating and was thoughtful.

"Your plan might work, Sandra. We could benefit. However, I need a moment to hash the idea around in my brain. Don't get me wrong, I am aware of the legal ramifications. It sounds like your women have been warned."

Sandra knew she should leave. There was one more item attached to her plan.

"Rather than sell this house, you might want to rent the house to receive additional income. I have a great realtor friend who may know someone in the area that does property rentals, placement, and management."

Fiona stirred sugar in her tea. Sandra handed her the creamer. Fiona poured the cream in her tea. She looked at the whirling mixture.

"I very much like the idea. This house was my husband's idea, rest his soul. I wanted a rambling ranch and he bought this monstrous two-story. You should see my master bedroom set. I'm a small person. He always went overboard. He made the fence outside for the entire backyard. I would have called contractors. Anyway, there's also a favor I want. I do need some help with my dress and shoes for the emerald show. A hairdresser might be required."

"I'll call Candy and have her fly here to measure you properly. She knows where to buy used designer dresses. She could also help in Las Vegas with getting you dressed. Candy has done women's hair and is a great escort if you need one."

"Good. Candy will work fine. Send her to me this week if she's not busy. Now, you mentioned something about promising investment opportunities."

Sandra took a deep breath.

"Let's not get ahead of ourselves. You've not told me about your answer to my first proposal."

The two women chatted for another hour.

Driving out of the expensive house gates, Sandra drove to a grocery store and pulled over. She wasn't sure if she should be elated or not. In the last minute of her visit, Fiona whispered to her.

"Count me in your game. The plan we discussed might work. You have better odds with me on board. I have some new tablecloths ordered. They are long and touch the floor. There's a bag by the pool door. You will need what is inside."

The change of plans was a risky one, riskier than the heist.

The old woman took the business card out of her purse with her lawyer's name and the paper with the date when the jeweler, Mr. Sloan, would examine the necklaces. Both were given to Sandra before she left the house.

There wasn't much time to complete the final pieces of this next phase.

3 Fall from Grace

Sandra Delray wrote in her notebook. She was alone. Remnants of her past were ditched for something better. Her old boring suits were sent to a charity. She bought expensive designer clothes and some one-piece stretch pantsuits with sturdy high heels with straps. She was in a better place now. You could say she was restored.

"Let's change restored to remarkable."

The trip to the casinos and the visit with Fiona were complete. There were some adjustments to make from her original plans.

Over a year ago, Sandra joined a second grief and support class for women. Before those classes, she tried therapy. She decided the therapists and counselors were using old techniques that didn't work for her. She was different. After taking some racing and skydiving lessons, she knew what she wanted.

"Excitement and riches are my focus and a better life. My brain knew I needed help but somehow, I found my true calling. Crossing the line was the new therapy. A person needed to know when to return without any consequences."

She saw five other women who were struggling with themselves and their therapy. They weren't moving forward. These women were more like she was at the beginning of her therapy.

Sandra developed their friendships and encouraged them to form their own group. They met at local coffee shops around Phoenix, Arizona. They talked about their dreams and skills. They didn't mind working for a living but wanted more time for fun. Sandra became their duly elected president.

The club consisted of an electrical engineer, a building inspector, a plumber, a welder, a banker, and a project manager.

Her contractor's job as a project manager was winding to a close. She smiled and thought about their last meeting.

"You know that we have a powerful table of women who could rob a bank or get away with a crime," said Sandra.

Darcy had laughed and grabbed another sugar packet.

"I love green money, but we need to think bigger."

Kim was super thin and looked at the almost empty coffee shop. She shouldn't drink coffee because the brew made her jittery. She wanted to be like other women. Kim drank coffee only when she was with them.

"I hear that emeralds make a woman forget about grief. I need about one hundred fifty pounds."

Candy appeared at the table with a large buttery croissant. The other women groaned when she smeared a huge pile of strawberry jam and cream cheese on top. She plunked a plain Greek yogurt down on the table. Her tight dress made her body look thinner.

Sandra knew Candy wasn't a good cook. The food was probably her breakfast, lunch, and dinner.

The mentioning of emeralds helped introduce an idea. Now was the time to involve her group in a well-conceived plan.

Sandra spoke. "There's an elderly actress who owns very large and real emeralds. These emeralds are from an era before man figured out how to make them in a lab. The emerald jewelry is loaded with equally impressive diamonds. Ms. Kendrell will be in Las Vegas in three months. There was a small article in the newspaper. The High Tower Plaza Hotel has booked her for a two-week show of her jewels and some other company's emeralds. I heard a rumor the Tiff Sander Jewelers is the participating firm. They will let Ms. Kendrell also wear some of their classy emerald collection while she is there."

Dawn and Danielle joined the meeting.

"Did we miss anything?"

Sandra looked at the women and went to the counter. She brought five croissants and plunked the jam and cream cheese packets in the center of the table. By the time she sat down, there was one croissant remaining. She ate a bite of the flaky bread.

"We talked about green emeralds and a possible heist. If we steal the emeralds, the question would be how do we sell them, and obtain the money?"

Dawn asked her, "Why would we want to sell them? I love emeralds and Candy does, too. Her hair clients wear the green-colored stone usually on their little finger."

Danielle made a grab for the extra strawberry jam from Dawn. "We sell them to purchase expensive houses near the beach or a chalet in ski country."

Kim brightened from the idea.

"I'd like to own a ranch somewhere in Wyoming."

Danielle appeared to be impressed. "Really? My theory about owning our own property is that we can watch the young men who frequent those types of places."

Kim took offense and stood up to leave. Danielle hit a sore spot. "God is that all you can think about is men. We women have agreed to *no men*. The club doesn't allow men. The heist is included within our club rules. None, zip, or you are out."

The women looked at Danielle.

"Well, I only want to look at them. Men don't break my concentration like some women I know."

"Kim, we've talked about the change that needs to happen in our lives. Everyone is stuck in loser mode. We want out. The plan is filled with risk. The odds are against us. Therefore, let's ensure the plan is doable," said Sandra.

Darcy volunteered to check the building rooms for access and safe areas. She would work with Dawn on building plans and any of the plumbing constraints. Danielle would review any electrical issues. Dawn also volunteered to look at the sewer diagrams and the heating vents because she was the smallest in their group. The size was important in case she needed to check the underground.

Candy would draw up the designs for
any cases or special bags. She was to find
out what materials they required. Kim would
find information about the very old wood-
topped vaults. They didn't want to be near
any area where there was real money. The
casino funds were watched more closely
than a guest's jewelry in the hotel.

Darcy asked, "Have you seen these
emerald pieces, Sandra?"

"Yes, quite a few of her collection
was viewed by me. She wore them
whenever I was visiting her nephew. There's
also a catalog from a show the woman was
involved in some years ago. I attended the
show. The jeweler is the same firm for the
next show."

Dawn was interested in jewelry.

"I'd like to see the catalog. I've
tinkered around with metal. I'm pretty good.
The shapes of the settings interest me and
the sizes of the rocks."

"I'll get you a copy and there needs
to be a change to our meeting place,"
commented Sandra.

She knew they would need to use
someone's house for any further meetings.
Darcy volunteered her home because her kid
graduated from college as a language
specialist and left home to work in a

government agency. Her kid lived in Miami and Darcy believed her home was safe from any future visitations.

The women next deposited their empty cups, packets, and napkins in the trash and left the shop.

Sandra drove Darcy back to her home and walked the perimeter of the house.

"You need a better security system and ditch the dining room drapes. Metal louvers should let light in but keep prying eyes out. Put a door in the dining room so we can close our drawings inside. Put a lock on one of the bedrooms as well as in the dining room. We'll store our tools and gear there until we can find a different spot. Have someone check your garage door opener. We might need a new one."

Darcy finished her list.

"We're really going to do this heist."

Sandra wasn't so sure.

"Let's wait and see what the other girls find for information. I'm going to a gem show and talk to dealers."

"Is a visit to a gem show really necessary? Oh, where is the gem show?"

"There's a large show in San Francisco on Friday and Saturday. Yes, I need to appear normal. I do know about jewelry and like gems. I've attended shows before."

Sandra went and waved goodbye to Darcy. She opened the door of her silver sports car and drove to her condominium. Looking at her bank account, she contacted a realtor. There was no need to own property.

She would stay at Darcy's place. The money from the condo would help purchase the necessary items for their activities.

Her green parakeet, Henri, would live at Darcy's house. She had called her veterinarian to schedule boarding services at their facility and find out rates for the future.

4 Men vs Women

Fiona liked men but she also supported women. Sandra told her a story about her women's club that convinced Fiona to join.

Sandra was an important person to Fiona. She saw the good heart buried inside. Sandra's spirit soared after they met as did Fiona's. Being around Sandra was always entertaining.

The club of women was a bunch of misfits who needed help. They needed a godmother with money so they could find their way.

Fiona stirred her tea as she recalled Sandra's story. She particularly liked the elephant part. Memories of her prior life caused her to make what she thought was a good decision. Fiona smiled remembering the story.

The six women's counselor from their grief and support class was gone. Another counselor made them write down ten words that evoked forgiveness. The assignment was mandatory.

The women voiced their unhappiness.

The whole idea of forgiveness was old-fashioned and usually backfired in a grief and support class. It wasn't that the women didn't believe in religion. They did.

The club women also learned previously from Sandra that their survival depended on getting past the lost phase. The group was into finding themselves. They were looking toward accomplishment goals instead. This last assignment irked their psyche. The women were better and didn't want to look back.

The counselor was a substitute for the day and clearly didn't understand this group of women. They were rejects beginning to feel courage big time.

Forgiveness was the last thing on their minds.

The substitute counselor left the room so they could write down words that popped into their conscious minds.

Darcy was the first Pitbull to object.

She jumped out of her chair knocking over her paper cup of coffee on the floor.

Kim grabbed some brown paper napkins and blotted the running liquid.

"This is bullshit. Who does she think we are? I'll tell her right now what popped into my mind."

The room was silent. Sandra said quietly.

"Darcy, please calm down. We aren't under attack. This is supposed to be a safe place."

She looked at Sandra. Sandra always encouraged Darcy and treated her as an equal. She slowly sat down.

"I'm sure this is our final assignment. I know we all hate this word. We've written the word on a piece of paper, thrown the paper in the woven garbage can, and lighted a huge bonfire. The garbage container blew up upon incineration. We cheered afterward and drank hot chocolate."

Darcy furiously started writing.

"I don't need to forgive the bitch."

Kim's claws came out. She corrected her, "You don't need to forgive anyone. It's not nice to call women bad names."

Sandra remembered that Kim dated men who never stayed around due to her overly critical nature. She corrected people's speech. The men couldn't handle a woman beating them up verbally. Kim joined their grief and support group to figure out what was wrong with her personality.

Darcy stopped writing. "How many dinosaurs can I remember how to spell? The big ones have larger poop. Let me think. There is Palaemastodon. That ought to fix my page for Missy Counselor. Five names are all I can muster."

Kim's face distorted. She looked at Sandra who shook her head. Kim knew Sandra didn't want to see fighting between them.

"The Palaemastoden is an early elephant. The dinosaurs were before the elephants."

"How do you know?" retorted Darcy.

"Honey, the dinosaurs died off. I read the book in the library. The elephants look different today from the earlier ones. I think the bush elephant's ears are larger than the ones in Asia. The females congregate in groups like us. They hear things we can't."

"Well, if they heard this conversation, the elephants would run into the hills."

Candy raised her hand timidly.

"I can't forgive someone who has not tried to correct a wrong. What if they make me send my list to my ex-boyfriend who stole my car? It took me three years to pay for the darn red sports car. I shouldn't have to apologize for his misdeeds. Besides, he doesn't understand the word forgiveness at all because he skipped church when he was little. Oh, I'm afraid of elephants. Don't scare me by mentioning running."

Dawn needed to intervene. Her ex-husband was a bigger fool by setting up a Ponzi scheme and used her as his partner.

"I spent two years in a woman's prison. There's no way I'm finishing this assignment. My hair was a mess from their watered-down prison shampoo. I agree with Candy. Thundering elephants shrieking is not a good image. Kim's correct, by the way, Darcy. I'm talking about the history lesson on elephants."

Danielle looked at Sandra. She took her piece of paper and ink pen. She started coloring the paper with tiny circles.

Sandra knew Danielle was counting the bruises she received from her old boyfriend before she went to a women's shelter to escape. Danielle started carrying a revolver in case she ran into another bad dude. She would blow the next creep to bits and be happy about it. Her theory was nice guys were rare and extinct like the dinosaurs.

The other women started talking all at once. Sandra let them grumble and finally interrupted her group. She took command of the meeting.

"Let's complete the assignment. I've sent you the synonym page for the word, forgiveness. Just copy the ten words down so we can end this last class. If the substitute

counselor makes us send the list to people
who tried to ruin our lives, we can be
creative. We switch the list and substitute a
blank page."

Darcy frowned, her own list
contained four dinosaurs and the elephant.

Sandra relented, "Darcy, you can use
whatever list you want. All of you can.
However, there are consequences to rattling
a cage with an angry bear inside. Maybe I
should have said elephant, but I like them.
The females are protective of their young. I
like the way the babies walk. There's a song
about their walk."

The other women listened to Sandra.

"We're a club now and we also need
to use our intelligence. We need to be
careful. If someone wants us to play mind
games, we turn ourselves into models as
pure as the snow. In other words, we fake it
until we make it."

Kim interjected, "Sandra is correct.
This whole counseling deal is part of our
training. Some of you were sent here by a
judge and must finish the course. We must
help each other to get a grip."

Danielle started whistling the baby
elephant song. The other women shook their
bodies in time to the music. They joined in
the whistling of the tune. The group settled

down and finished the assignment in five minutes.

The substitute counselor came back into the room. She heard the whistling and opened the door.

"My, aren't we a fun group!"

The substitute counselor collected their papers and read them. Five of the papers were identical. One of the papers was different. There were five names. One name was scratched out. There were six drawings of baby elephants.

The women looked at Darcy in amazement. They didn't know she could draw.

5 Interest in Craig

Sandra knew this emerald
business her club was planning would ruin
her ex-boyfriend's retirement plans if she
could pull the heist off. She counted on the
mission being successful.

Sandra looked at her perfectly
polished nails and toes.

"Timing is the key. Things should
unroll and unfold so slowly, there must
appear to be no connection to us."

Sandra looked at herself in the closet
door mirrors. The woman she saw was
different. The woman in the mirror looked
confident and beautiful. The scars didn't
show.

She dimmed the lights in her
bedroom, stepped out on Darcy's balcony,
and looked at the stars. Sandra was one of
those stars wandering through the sky. Her
private life was nonexistent.

"Someday there will be someone.
Not now, even though the handsome hotel
manager looked mighty interesting. He's
skilled and very comfortable around women.
I need to be careful around this one."

Sandra sighed. She was on a mission
of destruction if caught. The women in her

club were wonderful. Thinking about some of their required past meetings at the Grief and Loss Center, she suddenly laughed.

Sandra slowly turned. The night air inspired her to dream but it was time to go back inside. She locked the glass door and pulled the patio drapes. One by one, a piece of paper was taken out of her briefcase. The drawings were strewn in front of her in bits and pieces on the low console.

She kept rearranging the paper until she was satisfied. Her mind was clicking away. She hummed a tune. Music helped her think.

"My violin needs a new string."

Even her girls didn't know the final plans. Fiona befriended her when she needed someone. She shook her head. Sandra knew she would never betray Fiona, especially now.

The first phase was already completed in that the building plans of the casinos were reviewed. The second phase was casing the casinos which they already did. The third step was the emeralds and the show. Here was where Sandra again paused.

There was no need to change anything. The girls would perform, and she would continue to lead.

All the women agreed that the money from this heist was worth the effort.

If they could do the heist, they could continue to live their lives in a much richer way.

The only original club members who wanted to move to Europe after the heist were Sandra and Danielle. The other women would either stay or find new locations to live.

The first inspection of the Splendor and Devon Casino area was complete. They checked out the other place where the emeralds were to be displayed at the High Tower Plaza Hotel.

"Why am I still struggling? Because you could be convicted, Sandra. What you are planning is a crime!"

Her mind wandered back to Craig Connor. She recognized her heart did a little skip when he looked at her. There was a moment she couldn't explain away.

"I should kiss him and get over this feeling. He probably is not a good kisser."

She toyed with one of the papers on the console table. Sandra peeked out the window. The streetlight was green. The rain started falling.

"Sandra, girl, you are wrong. You can always tell. Craig will be excellent at kissing."

The rainwater was running down the street.

"He won't ever understand the heist. You must forget about Mr. Connor. No pursuit is necessary and recommended. Plus, no more flirting in front of the security cameras."

Sandra also liked men. There was a difference between men and women. This difference could be a big mistake.

6 Dawn's Work

Sandra drove to Dawn's house in Phoenix two weeks after her visit with Fiona in LA.

"Dawn, please open the door. I need to know how the jewelry pieces are coming along."

She could hear some metal on metal filing. The sound stopped. Dawn looked through the peephole, unlocked the door, and let her friend inside.

"Sorry, I needed to get this one clasp to work properly. I heard you yelling. It's a good thing my neighbors live a block away. I love this old jewelry. The maker in New York City was brilliant. I've removed the rocks and washed them. The metal takes longer and requires fine brushes. We don't want any fingerprints or DNA to appear on them other than the jeweler's company agent. I assumed she handled and possibly wore some of the pieces."

Sandra looked at the trays of empty settings numbered along with the appropriate stones.

"Yes, she did wear some of the larger pieces. You were wise to clean them. We can't have any slipup plus the jewels need to sparkle. How soon can we have them back? The pieces need to be ready in fifteen days."

Sandra looked at her calendar.

"Also, the box needs to be perfect in case Fiona's plan folds. Here are the new velvet cases. She will simply explain the old velvet deteriorated when the jeweler arrives at her home."

Dawn struggled to look at her wall calendar.

"I've checked the company's website and talked with a person at their 800 number for the absolute correct dimensions. Not to worry, I called from a phone at the library while Kim distracted the man. They still used a landline. I'm struggling with the logo stamp."

Sandra tapped her fingers on the table. The tapping matched a drum sound. Dawn knew Sandra was getting impatient about this part of the process. She knew Sandra was also thinking very fast.

"Do you need Danielle's help?"

Dawn frowned. She preferred to work alone. She counted the hours she could work. The timing was tight.

"Sure, send her over."

Sandra texted Danielle that Dawn missed her. That was their code for top priority.

Danielle texted back, "Aw, I miss my twin, too."

Sandra sent a text to Candy for the urgent dress and shoe shopping spree expedition required by Fiona. She included the idea of being an escort and helping Fiona get dressed while in Las Vegas. Also, her beauty shop skills were urgently required. The request was to help her dear friend who found shopping and zippers more difficult as she aged. She explained about the dead hairdresser.

Candy responded, "I would love to help Ms. Fiona Kendrell. I'll call the shop that I know in Los Angeles so they can put some dresses aside. I'm glad Ms. Kendrell gave you her petite dress size and shoe size. This should be easy. I'll make sure the woman looks elegant. The new chemicals the beauticians use is usually a little better. Thank you for thinking about me."

Putting her cell back inside her purse, Sandra glanced at the case.

She wasn't worried about the text to Candy. If questioned, the text would solidify the reason Candy was chosen as Ms. Kendrell's escort.

7 Fiona and Candy

Candy was met by Ms. Kendrell at the Used and Glam Designer store in LA. Fiona changed her mind and wanted to see more than dresses. Ms. Kendrell needed to update her wardrobe.

"Hello, Candy, this is my butler and chauffeur, Jarret. He will give me the high-five sign as will you when there is something worthy of us purchasing."

Candy shook hands with Jarret who wore a twinkle in his eye. He recognized a pretty woman right away. Candy knew the look. Men fell in love with her immediately. She bowed to Jarret.

A salesclerk appeared and took them to a private room. Fiona and Jarret settled in comfortable chairs with hot tea.

The models came out wearing three outfits. The first one was a gray lace ensemble top and skirt. The skirt showed an elastic waist and flared downward. The top underneath was peach silk lining which looked illuminated. The second was the same dress designer with a black stretch three-piece outfit with silver threads. The third was a green velvet jacket with a green skirt with large gold and white flowers on an emerald green background.

"I want to take all three dressy outfits home to try on later. Now, do you have any comfortable pant outfits that don't look like sweats?"

The saleswoman and models disappeared. The models changed and walked back out into the small private room.

Fiona checked eight of the ten outfits. She and her butler-chauffeur left the store.

Candy wrung up the items on her charge card and drove to the old woman's house in Los Angeles. She was expected to stay overnight and stay for two days. In the morning, she was surprised to see Fiona in the kitchen eating pancakes and sausage.

"I couldn't sleep last night. I was too excited. I need to try on the gowns first," said Fiona.

Jarret handed Candy a warm plate of pancakes, sausage, and a glass of orange juice.

"Can you do hair?"

Candy swallowed her huge bite and said, "Yes. I used to be a beautician in my former life when I owned a red car."

"I heard about the man who stole your vehicle. Don't worry because he's walking now wearing ugly shoes. I'm glad you are a beautician. Maybe tomorrow, we can do my hair. I'm in great need. I expect we'll be friends if you can fix this ugly permanent some off-the-wall new person gave me. She showed cheap tattoos on her arm. The woman might as well have used a magic marker."

Candy wasn't going to tell the old woman about her butterfly tattoo on her left foot. The image was now blurry. The object looked like a bug. She was thinking about removal.

"Of course, I need to order some beauty products online. They will ship overnight."

Candy disappeared to get on her computer.

"Thank, God, Jarret. We have found someone who understands us!"

Jarret smiled. He was looking forward to seeing the changeover for his employer. He left the room to make their arrangements for the limousine to drive Fiona and Candy to Las Vegas. His boss wanted to see some of the landscape. Their return trip would be by air.

8 Arrival in Las Vegas

The Splendor and Devon Casino was almost devoid of people at three o'clock in the afternoon. The hotel was older, much like the hotel across the street. The carpet was cleaned and washed regularly. The hotel smelled good. There was a small florist shop on the property.

The manager, Craig Connor looked at the security screens with Kevin Meadow, his security agent.

"The floor appears to be pretty quiet. Where are the Las Vegas tourists?"

Both men watched the camera in the Green Room.

"Hold it right there," said Craig.

Kevin saw the blonde woman.

"Ms. Delray must like us. She's back and looking mighty fine in her gray business suit with red heels and a matching purse."

Craig frowned.

"Why is she here?"

Kevin looked at his boss. "Vacation, sir? She looks relaxed and serene. Ms. Delray might have business interests here. I would hire her."

Craig zoomed the screen.

"That is exactly why I'm worried. The woman is up to something."

Now it was Kevin's turn to screw up his face.

"I see she has definitely drawn a reaction from you. Maybe your heart is doing flipflops due to overwork. You get to see but can't touch. Too bad."

"I get to meet people all the time. Shaking hands and buying priority clients lunch is part of my job."

Craig sat down in the chair to watch Sandra. He didn't see any of her friends.

"What time did she check into our hotel?"

Kevin went to the computer and typed the woman's name.

"She is in Room 141 on Fourth Floor overlooking the side street and checked in about two fifteen today."

Craig looked at the computer to verify the information for himself. The last time, the woman stayed in three of their elegant rooms with her friends. He wondered why the change.

"Ms. Delray has won another game of cards in our Green Room. I wonder who taught her. She's good at poker. Her face doesn't give her away. The question is what else is she good at that could be a problem for this hotel?"

"Now boss, I think you are overreacting. There she is leaving the card table and is looking at a text on her cell phone. I consider those moves normal behavior for a female tourist in our fair city."

Craig grabbed his jacket.

"I'm going to follow her. The woman gives me tingles down my spine whenever I see her. Everything around her appears magnified. I'm afraid that the sky might fall any minute. There is danger in the air. I can smell it. There's a weird feeling when she moves her head of hair."

"Somehow, boss, you are seeing and feeling more than I am. Are you sure you don't have a fever?"

Craig cranked, "No, I just can't see the problem that's coming."

Kevin shrugged his shoulders and shook his head as his boss left the security room. He didn't feel any danger. He thought his manager might need a vacation.

"Skies falling and hair moving did sound crazy. Tingling happened to me when I met my wife."

Eating his roast beef sandwich, Kevin watched Mr. Connor follow Ms. Delray out the door. He switched cameras to the front of the building and watched them

both enter the High Tower Plaza Hotel
lobby in a single file.

"Shoot, if I was her, I'd head to the
bar," said Kevin. "They must be serving
afternoon appetizers by now. I like those hot
chicken wings with the white beef puffs.
Then, there are the gooey crispy cheese
drops with scallions. Man, I wish I worked
at the other casino. We don't serve
appetizers for free in this hotel. That's why
we don't have customers in the afternoon."

Kevin was so busy thinking about
food, he missed one of their security guards
letting in some workers from the Johnson
Water Heater Company.

He used the computer to adjust one
of the cameras near the front door.

9 Fiona, Candy, & Sandra

The two women were waiting for her in the restaurant. There was a large plate of steaming appetizers from the bar area on their table.

"Hello, Fiona, I'm so glad to see you have made the limousine ride in good time."

Fiona was eating some buffalo wings. The cook was trying a new recipe. Candy smiled and signaled the waiter for more iced tea.

Fiona wiped her hands on the small moist towelette. She smiled mischievously.

"Mr. Sloan helped me with my tea water."

Sandra brightened.

"Yes, I received Candy's brief text. I need to congratulate you on pulling off the coup of the century. Fiona, you missed your calling and should have gone into politics. Imagine how much trouble you could have caused using your deception skills. Let's not mention your communication skills which are top-notch."

"Thank you, my dear. Years and years of time practicing does make wheels turn. Or should I say, a certain person's eyes might have been diverted? You'll get there."

Candy's eyes gleamed.

Sandra read the brief text.

"Our people have arrived at the other hotel and their job has begun."

Candy and Fiona knew she meant Dawn, Kim, and Darcy arrived.

The three women raised their free glass of an ice cream drink. An elderly gentleman bought them once he saw Fiona. They clinked the glass objects in a salute.

The man at the bar watched in silence as he saw the odd combination of women at the table in the restaurant. He was sitting near the opening into the lounge. He asked the bartender,

"Do you know the elderly gendarme?"

The bartender looked.

"Not sure Mr. Connor. The elderly gentleman left after talking with her. I see another woman is at the table. They look like they are enjoying themselves. The first two have only been in the restaurant for about an hour."

Candy could feel someone staring at her. She bent down to slide her bag toward Sandra. Sandra did the same with her empty bag.

Comfortable that her part was completed, Candy twisted her ponytail to put Sandra on high alert. Candy shook her hair free and redid the hairband.

"My hair today sticks to my neck like glue. I need to change my outfit."

Sandra and Fiona were slowly eating the appetizer.

Fiona said, "It's the stiffener in the collar of my blouses that bugs me. I used to be able to wear low necklines when I was younger. Nowadays, old women want to put a scarf around their neck to keep the breeze from blowing down to their underwear. I prefer necklaces."

Sandra let out a chuckle. She knew Candy bought Fiona some new undergarments. The old woman picked the popular rose-beige color.

Candy looked directly at Craig Connor. Immediately, she knew the man followed Sandra and was now keenly watching her.

Candy thought the other hotel manager, Mr. Connor, being in the restaurant this time of day was a little odd. She didn't say anything or do anything further to see if the man would make any move toward them.

Fiona noticed the young man in the bar. She turned her attention to Sandra and became the actress she was in the past. Distraction was necessary.

"I absolutely love my gowns we brought for the events. I feel like I did when I was on the stage. Oh, the crowds that came to see our shows were warm and friendly. Their clapping was wonderful to hear at the end. I miss those days. However, this last emerald show is going to be the very best one. The emeralds are dim compared to the recognition and meeting of new people. This show has gotten me out of my dreary house and lifted my spirits. I cannot thank you enough for helping me get my act together."

Sandra only half listened and was acutely aware of Candy's silence. Sandra touched Candy's hand. Candy hid her hand and pointed toward the bar. Sandra moved the identical bag out of view and pushed the object under her side of the table.

A man slowly approached their section. He appeared to be listening to Fiona's conversation as he stopped at their table.

"Hello, ladies, I thought I should welcome you back to Las Vegas."

Sandra took a second to cover her anger. She shouldn't have checked into his hotel.

"Yes, Mr. Connor, it is very nice to be in Las Vegas again. I am surprised to see you at your competitor's hotel."

"I need to check out their free appetizer buffet. My chefs have been pushing me to offer some similar items. I heard from the bartender someone beat me in offering you a free drink. I'll be faster next time."

Sandra stood up, "Forgive me, I should introduce you to my friends. You know Candy Evans from Phoenix. She has stayed at your hotel before. The other woman is an old friend of mine, Ms. Fiona Kendrell from Los Angeles. We decided to try the appetizers here and we give our wholehearted approval."

Craig shook Fiona's frail hand and Candy's. Fiona didn't mention their prior meeting. He was going to offer his hand to Sandra except she bent to pick up her bag.

"I do have to run and get some things I forgot to bring along. Bye, Candy and Fiona."

The two women nodded their goodbyes.

Craig was quick. "Let me escort you back to my hotel."

Sandra found no way to get out of his suggestion. She let him take her elbow and walk her toward the other hotel lobby.

Candy looked at Fiona. Fiona took a sip of her iced tea and selected the gooey food item.

"I wish that I was young again. I would give Sandra a run for her money over that young man."

Candy couldn't help but giggle. She knew Sandra could handle her own way with the likes of a possible man venturing close to their club.

"The manager of the other hotel across the street is very perceptive. I think he likes Sandra," said Candy.

"Yes, Sandra could wear heavy overhauls and he would notice her walk. He appreciates a good female specimen. His eyes gave him away and the way he tried to take command. I love it when men are in the dark. Men take baby elephant steps and women run like gazelles on the open plain."

Candy wondered and voiced her opinion.

"Craig is a full-grown elephant."

Fiona looked wistful.

"I went to Africa for my wedding and honeymoon. We had a ball on a safari. The Ngoma drum sound is much better in person. The museum recorders don't do the instrument justice. Someday both you and Sandra will go to Tanzania, too."

Candy signed the restaurant bill for the iced teas. She wasn't sure she wanted to go to Africa. The man she was with would probably steal her gazelle or run her over with a huge ten-thousand-pound elephant."

Fiona noticed Candy's silence about her comments.

"I promise you, Candy girl, life is going to take you for a joyous ride. Some of the tour guides in Africa are a lot of fun. The doctors are especially nice if you get ill."

Candy didn't know what to say.

"I'm sure you are what my women's club would call a very romantic and eccentric woman who enjoys pretty underwear."

Fiona grinned thinking about her romantic thoughts. Men were useful to have around. However, she was getting old and eccentric. Jarret told her every day those two words. Still, she remembered vividly the past and the current events. Her mind hadn't decayed yet.

Candy grabbed her black bag. "We should see if they have put our luggage in the room. I'm needing to work on my computer again."

Fiona stood while Candy wheeled the portable wheelchair close. Fiona didn't have to walk so far.

"The food and excitement have made me a little tired. Will you let Jarret know we arrived safely?"

"I already sent him a text message while we waited for the rental car. He texted back that you should enjoy yourself."

"I plan on enjoying every moment. He must miss me."

The elderly woman and her escort went to their double suite of rooms.

10 Water Heater Problem

Craig escorted Ms. Delray through the lobby of the Splendor and Devon Casino when he was suddenly paged over the loudspeaker by his security man.

"Ms. Delray, I'm so sorry. Something has come up. Maybe we can do dinner while you are here during your stay. I'll call you or better yet, I have your room number."

Sandra was relieved. The mold problem on the wallboard surrounding the water heater for the hotel's small classroom kitchen must have been found by Darcy and the plumbing company in Las Vegas. The hotel across the street was the same configuration for classes.

"No problem, I understand your duties keep you very busy."

Craig frowned as Sandra walked away toward the elevator that would take her to her room. The woman hadn't given him a positive affirmation about a future dinner date.

"Kevin, what the heck is so important that you needed to page me. I'm in the middle of talking with one of our guests. This interruption must be very important."

Kevin saw the two people walk through the front door of the lobby. He should have waited. Now his boss was in a foul mood because of him. He wondered if the mold was tiny or huge. Maybe Kevin should have asked a guard to check how large the mold pattern was on the wallboard in the tiny room next to the classroom kitchen.

Darcy went back to the Johnson Water Heater Company truck and waited for the two men on the project to explain to the manager at the Splendor and Devon Casino the mold problem and how dangerous mold was in any structure. The mold would need to be removed immediately. The wallboard needed to be trashed. Next, the old water heater that didn't work would need to be removed.

While in the company truck, Darcy texted Dawn and Kim to see if they arrived with the vendor hot dog motor vehicle for the street fair space.

Darcy sent the note, "Hi, did you arrive?"

Dawn texted and copied Sandra, "Yes, we're fine."

Sandra sat on her hotel bed and sent a text to Kim to make sure the changes were made to the booth and did she remember to purchase the hot dog stuff?

Sandra's note read, "You've made the journey to Las Vegas?"

Kim's response was, "Yes, perfectly."

Sandra knew the stage was ready. Darcy went last week on a call to the High Tower Plaza Hotel. There was a leaky pipe. A temporary fix was placed on their pipe until parts could be ordered.

The heist team was positioned. Sandra could hear the music play in her head when she performed in the orchestra years ago.

"The violin and drum section have started their music."

Sandra took a quick shower and laid out her dress for the evening. Her job was important. She was to be in the Gambling Room playing cards this evening at the High Tower Plaza Hotel to see when the armored vehicle arrived with Fiona's emeralds. Those emeralds would be placed in the hotel guest security until Sunday morning. The shipment's safe deposit needed to be verified.

There was a knock at her door. She quickly grabbed the hotel robe with her wet blonde hair draping down her back and answered the door.

There was a hotel person with a large bouquet of flowers and a fruit basket. Sandra opened the door wider to let the person deposit the gifts. She looked up to see the hotel manager's eyes.

"Mr. Connor?"

Sandra was speechless. Her brain was racing forward.

"Craig, please. I feel we have stepped past the formal part. *You look amazingly wet and supremely healthy.* You're also wearing one of our signature robes. We should have our marketing people catch your surprised and very wet look."

Sandra quickly recovered when the hotel person walked out of the doorway.

"You mentioned something previously about dinner?"

"Yes, are you available this evening around eight o'clock? I would enjoy your conversation this evening."

Sandra looked into Craig's eyes. There was no quick excuse for the moment hitting her brain. She suddenly realized her hair was a mess and she didn't have any makeup on. The robe was a last-minute thing. He knew the robe was carelessly thrown onto her body in order to answer the door. She pulled the robe a little tighter.

She was taking too long to answer. Craig needed to encourage her to come.

"Well, let me see if this will help your decision. Our lobster is especially good this evening in case you are interested."

"How about the hotel's filet mignon? I like to sink my teeth into things."

Craig took the bait. He moved a little closer. She stepped back. He hesitated. There would be plenty of time later to get to know her.

"The filet mignon is worthy, I promise. If not, I'll cook one for you myself."

Sandra didn't want him to cook her anything.

"Restaurant food is fine. I'll meet you on the top floor next to the entrance."

Craig smiled.

"I'll come to your door like a proper gentleman."

Sandra needed to concede and close her door. The floor she was standing on was dripping wet.

"I'll be ready."

Craig couldn't resist. He saw the two evening gowns on the bed.

"The red one looks nice."

Sandra blinked. He caught her again by surprise. She closed the door softly and turned the lock.

Craig walked away whistling.

She stood behind the closed door for fifteen minutes. Her brain was replaying the drill in her head. Craig just interrupted the heist.

"This dinner might work to my advantage. Danielle will need to monitor the job until I can take over."

Sandra stepped out onto the balcony and made the phone call.

"I have a date tonight and won't be able to join you. Perhaps you can take my place at cards."

Sandra waited. Danielle would know there was a problem she couldn't get out of for the evening.

"As long as he's dark, tall and handsome?"

Sandra looked at the street below that was blocked off for the street fair. She pondered her reply. All texts and phone conversations must not give away their plans.

"Yes, on a high scale."

She waited for two minutes.

"Fine."

Sandra went inside to dry her hair and get dressed for the evening. She looked at the two gowns on her bed.

"Red is the gown that I'll wear tonight. The gown is exactly the dress for a little danger. The purple one is not hot enough to make a man forget and throw caution to the wind."

Sandra took the purple gown and placed it inside a plastic bag. She answered her door and handed the gown to Candy to wear for the Friday affair with the Tiff Sander Jewelers and Ms. Kendrell.

11 Dinner with Craig

A light tap on Sandra's door made her aware that Craig Connor was waiting. She opened the door and let him into her room.

Craig blinked and was stunned. The blonde woman turned, and her hair spun in the air. She looked like the picture. Her hair was long with curls and her dress was fringed with crisscrosses of fabric on her bodice. The skirt draped and hugged her figure.

"The red dress works. Your hair is amazing and I'm starving."

He took Sandra's jacket and helped her put her arms in the sleeves. Then they rode the elevator to the restaurant at the top of the hotel. The hostess escorted them to a private table with a view of the downtown Las Vegas lights.

"This is a beautiful view. Your guests can see for miles."

The waiter approached. Craig asked her one question.

"Red or white?"

Sandra looked up at the young male waiter.

"House white wine is okay."

74

The waiter looked at Craig. Craig told the waiter the year, wine chateau name, and type. The waiter disappeared and returned with their glasses and wine. He poured a sample for Craig who nodded the wine was fine.

Sandra tasted her drink.

"This is very good."

"It should be. The bottle is about one hundred fifty dollars."

Sandra blinked. The rest of the meal was very excellent and pricey. They talked about their past and where they grew up. The conversation was normal first date stuff.

Craig made her laugh. She felt alive listening to him tell stories about his hotel. The three hours passed quickly. Sandra looked at her clock. She was overdue on her check-in with the club women.

"This dinner has been fabulous except I must get back to my room. I have some additional work to do this evening."

Craig understood and walked her back to her hotel room. At the last minute, she relented and invited him inside her room for coffee.

While she was preparing the brew, Craig came over and took her in his arms and kissed her. Sandra responded. They held each other close and were venturing further into their exploration of more soft kisses. There was a light knock at Sandra's door.

"Saved by a knock on the door," exclaimed Craig.

He released Sandra and opened the door. He saw Sandra's friend, Danielle, with a roller suitcase, a violin case, and a very large purse. Large purses seemed to be in vogue this year.

"Hi, Mr. Connor, isn't it? I'm sorry but the violin won't fit in your nice guest vaults in guest security. I needed to lug the instrument with me. Sandra, I'm sorry about arriving late. I got carried away at the High Tower Plaza Hotel playing the cards and later slots with Candy."

Craig stepped aside and Sandra helped her with the violin case. There was a dead silence.

"Well, ladies, I need to bid both of you a very good evening."

He stepped toward Sandra and whispered, "I'll talk to you tomorrow."

Sandra closed the door. Danielle sat down on the couch in the room. There were massive questions in her eyes. The women agreed to no men until the heist and the money was passed around.

"I couldn't get out of dinner. The man is very persistent."

Danielle knew they were leaving at five o'clock in the morning.

Sandra sat down on the couch.

"Did the women complete their jobs?"

"Yes. The hotdog stand was a success. Kim and Dawn were able to undo the manhole. They placed the portable ladder from the food truck in the underground sewer where you suggested. We left a glove further down the street close to the High Tower Plaza Hotel. The door in the one hotel was unlocked and they were going to jimmy the other hotel door. There were old marks. The door didn't need much coaxing to leave it slightly ajar. The water heater installation and new wallboard are completed at the Splendor and Devon Casino. Dawn accessed the hotel and crawled along the heating ducts to the show hotel's Guest Secure Item area. Another glove was left on the heating duct."

"Everything has gone as planned."

Danielle looked at Sandra.

"Yes, but what will happen when Mr. Connor finds out you have disappeared?"

Sandra took her small diamond earrings off and laid them on the table.

"I can't worry about Mr. Connor's reaction. Friday evening is when Fiona meets with the jewelers, hotel sponsors, and press for a gala dinner. We must not remain in Las Vegas."

Danielle went into the bedroom. Sandra unzipped her dress. She went into the bathroom and took the robe from the hook. Then she remembered the coffee. Sandra poured herself a cup and sat down on the couch for a long night. She couldn't sleep.

Sandra heard Danielle close the bedroom door.

"Sleep avoids those with reckless hearts. I never expected this reaction. Why did I kiss him? Whew, my guard was dropped. The timing is so very bad. Craig might be a problem in the future."

Sandra wondered how long it would take the jewelers to realize Fiona's collection of gems wasn't real. The police would be called, and every stone would be overturned to find the gems and criminals.

The insurance company would eventually have to pay the insured amount. The insurance company would blame the transport company and the hotel. There would be an agent sent to investigate.

She heard the music playing in her head. The sound was soothing. She played her violin in her head to the notes.

"Someday I will play this song with an orchestra. The question is where will the location be? Rome might work."

Sandra knew the original beautiful emerald gems were secure. She folded her red gown and jacket. She pulled the suitcase out of the closet and added the clothes with her shoes. The case was zippered shut. She set the alarm on her phone. Slowly, she drifted asleep.

Sandra heard her phone buzzing. She felt the time that passed was mere minutes. Danielle was waiting for her to get dressed. Danielle held the rental car keys in her hands. There was no time for breakfast.

The two women exited the hotel without any mishap. They climbed into the rental car and drove to Los Angeles to a bank lockbox.

By the time Craig Connor knew Sandra was gone, the two women were on an airplane to New York City and eventually Rome.

Sandra saw his text messages on the drive to their hotel room in New York City. She would wait and call him back.

"It was a good thing that I told him someday I wanted to live in Rome during dinner. All I need to do is tell him the opportunity presented itself sooner than I expected."

Sandra worried the man might follow her. She expressed her thoughts to Danielle.

"What do I do if Craig runs into me again? He will probably be suspicious. The heist will be all over the news."

Danielle waited for the turn in the freeway before she responded.

"You must fake things like always."

Sandra didn't feel very happy about her friend's response. She knew that she was to blame if exposure happened.

"If there are any issues, I'll deal with them my way."

Danielle glanced at the map on the console. They were close to the hotel in New York City. The two women didn't speak further until dinner. Danielle ordered Chinese food. She told Sandra this type of food was loaded with anti-depressants.

Danielle left the room so that Sandra could place her phone call in privacy.

Sandra talked with Craig for almost an hour. He was extremely unhappy with her leaving without telling him. He called her a few names. That's when she hung up. He called her back and apologized.

He sounded contrite when he told her, "Look, I get controlling and overreactive. I'm upset we didn't have another evening together. We needed more time to get to know each other. One kiss wasn't enough. Call me when you get settled in Rome."

Sandra chose to agree with Craig, or the call wouldn't end anytime soon. Danielle stepped back into their hotel room. Sandra nodded that her call was completed.

Danielle sat on the bed next to Sandra and hugged her friend.

"Do you think Henri will be okay in quarantine?"

Danielle shook her head in relief. Thoughts of men left her dear friend. She was concentrating on something that loved her more. "Henri will be fine at the veterinarian until you can bring him to Europe."

Sandra watched Danielle go into the bathroom. She touched her lips. Craig was an excellent kisser.

"Wrong, he was hot."

12 Emerald Show Receptions

Fiona watched as Candy finished her hairdo. Holding the mirror, the old woman saw the puffy curls. The hairdo was perfect. Candy lightly sprayed the woman's hair to hold the set.

The two women went to the elevator and descended to the first floor of the High Tower Plaza Hotel for the Tiff Sander Jewelers Emerald Show. Fiona wore a beautiful five-carat necklace surrounded by diamonds and smaller emerald cut earrings courtesy of the jeweler.

This evening show was in a separate room from the consumer show scheduled for a start date on Sunday. Showcasing the jewelry store's emeralds on Friday evening would allow the commercial buyers to place their annual order of emerald jewelry.

There were pictures taken at the show of Ms. Kendrell wearing their diamonds. Candy stayed out of the spotlight in the purple gown while wearing her guest's badge. The refreshments and food were located outside in the courtyard surrounded by heavy security for the event.

Ms. Kendrell was visited by some elderly women who wanted to meet her. She was pleased to talk to the many women about where they lived and what they did during the day. Fiona remembered the names of the Las Vegas high society women and the clubs they belonged to. She was particularly interested in the garden club and talked profusely about her rare roses in California.

By eleven o'clock in the evening, the patrons dwindled as the jewelers were completing their orders. Fiona allowed the jeweler's assistant to remove their jewels from her person. She would wear a different set for the Saturday brunch scheduled the next day at noon. She and Candy went to their room to retire.

The next day was a repeat of the prior evening except the brunch was smaller. The two women left the luncheon at two in the afternoon to pack. Their flight was scheduled to leave for California before six.

Ms. Kendrell was not required to attend her section of the emerald show. Her picture would be a large cardboard display at the entrance to the second room.

They traveled home to LA and were picked up at the airport by Jarret. Candy would stay until Monday and return to Phoenix.

Candy contacted Sandra who put the call on speaker status so Danielle could also listen.

Candy told them the affair was exceptionally fun for Fiona and her portrait would look fantastic with the emerald collection. She was sorry she would miss the show but needed to return to her day job in Phoenix.

Sunday morning, the viewing of Fiona's emeralds was delayed because the pipe repair failed, and water leaked onto the floor. Emergency plumbers were called. They retrieved the new part from the manager of the Johnson Water Heater Company. The manager called Darcy to find out where the package was located. The package was in the company's mailroom.

13 Fiona's Gem Show

The thirty-five million-dollar collection of emerald jewelry and diamonds was opened to the public at noon on Monday. The head jeweler from the Tiff Sander Jewelers left his assistant in charge of the show. A map of the jewelry and the secured cases was given to the assistant. The assistant filled the cases.

Jim Sloan smiled. The emeralds were placed in their tall locked glass cases. The flowers arrived and the special lighting arrived in the morning. The cardboard photograph of Ms. Kendrell was placed outside the room door. There were velvet roped areas for people to walk past the jewelry. The guards were at their stations.

The time was fifteen minutes before showtime when the head jeweler examined the floor with the hotel manager.

"This looks stunning, Mr. Sloan. I'm glad you decided to use our hotel again for your store's show and Ms. Kendrell's show. The line of people out front and the media vans are a testament to the emerald's popularity and your firm's good name."

"We strive to do our best. My people are committed to doing a good job."

"Did you want to preview Ms. Kendrell's collection before we allow the public inside?"

"Mr. Stark, I've seen her gems many times before. We can let the media group that you've chosen take a picture of the room for their newspaper and then we'll let the general public inside.

Dwayne Stark waved at the newspaper manager, Quinn Turner, to allow his photographer to take pictures of the room. He took a few closeups of the larger emerald displays. They received the writeup and history of the emeralds Ms. Kendrell prepared earlier.

Ms. Kendrell's husband traveled frequently to Zambia in the 1940s and bought many emeralds from the locals and later more emeralds in the 1950s. He then joined the team of engineers building a dam in the area. He preferred buying emeralds that were uncut. He would take the stones to his favorite jewelry cutter in New York City to fashion and polish the cuts for jewelry. The jewels were high in chromium and needed to be cut perfectly to show their refractive brilliancy. He purchased the diamonds in New York from various jewelers who would give him a good deal.

Quinn looked at the images on his photographer's camera. He showed them to Dwayne Stark.

"Those pictures look mighty good to me. What do you think, Jim?"

Jim glanced at the pictures. He started to speak and looked again at display number fourteen. The large emerald wasn't flat enough on the velvet board.

"The pictures are fine."

Mr. Turner and his photographer left the room to head toward their van. Jim Sloan signaled his assistant.

"We need to unlock number fourteen and lay the large emerald down better. Please notify the security guard."

The security guard with the display keys unlocked the number fourteen display. Mr. Sloan maneuvered the large emerald so that the stone was flat. He readjusted the light on the necklace and stopped.

Mr. Sloan took out his jewelry lens and examined the stone. He looked toward the door where the lines of people were waiting. He motioned for the security guard to open three more cases. Those cases were examined. His mouth was dry, and he started shaking.

Mr. Sloan felt faint. His eyes bulged and he fell over onto the marble floor. His head started bleeding. Jim tried to speak, but no words came out. He was struggling with a stroke.

The hotel manager shouted to his security people to lock the doors and call an ambulance. The security guard relocked the open display cases of emeralds and diamonds.

Jim Sloan was taken away in an ambulance to the nearest hospital.

The emerald show was canceled for Monday until further notice. The hotel would need to wait until another jeweler from Tiff Sander Jewelers could arrive.

A few security guards were left in place to guard the emeralds and diamonds in the room.

The newspaper did run the pictures and Fiona's article in their newspaper with the closure of the show due to Mr. Sloan's illness. They hoped the show would reopen later. The newspaper would continue to follow the story for their readers.

A day later Mr. Sloan passed away. The Tiff Sander Jewelers decided to cancel the Fiona Kendrell portion of the show due to such dire circumstances. Jim Sloan's assistant was given the task of repacking the jewels in their special box and handing them over to the transport company.

Mr. Dwayne Stark was glad to get the more expensive valuables out of his hotel, especially if there would be no additional income from the show.

The transport company notified Fiona of when her jewels would be delivered to her home in Los Angeles. She called the Tiff Sander Jewelers with her lawyer. They wanted to receive not only her jewels back but compensation for her share of the lost revenue from the tickets to her portion of the show.

The jewelers assured Fiona they would comply.

When Fiona returned home, she sat for a few moments to get her breath.

"I need to call Candy. I lost the beauty operator's card she gave me."

Jarret gave her the cell phone.

Candy immediately picked up the call.

"I'm unsure about my hair person. I think losing her card was meant to be. Call it divine providence."

Candy knew Fiona wasn't talking about the beautician. She talked briefly with Candy about the recent episodes in the newspaper.

"I do have another beautician who might work out better for you. I'll text you with her name, phone number, and address."

89

Fiona rambled on about her hair for five more minutes. Then she mentioned the show cancellation and how she was upset by the recent turn of events.

"You stay strong. There is always good happening in the future."

"I'll try. I feel sad that Mr. Sloan has passed. However, my jewelry is coming home. I asked my lawyer to be here when they arrive. He has my list and photos of the collection. He can help me examine and make sure the twenty pouches are accounted for. My eyesight sometimes is blurry."

"Good idea. If you need anything, Fiona, I'm here for you. Sandra and Danielle are in Rome, but they are only a call away."

"Thank you, dear. It's nice to have such good friends."

14 Return of Emeralds

The transport firm arrived at Fiona Kendrell's home. The large jewelry box was brought into her home and set upon the round table. A different guard was working on return transport delivery.

Sitting at the table was the Tiff Sander Jeweler's new head jeweler, Rowan Edward along with Fiona's lawyer, Horatio Golden.

The tea cart sat in the corner.

"Would you like any refreshments, gentlemen?"

The men declined. Jarret handed Fiona a bottle of apple juice. Her hands were a little shaky. Her lawyer jumped up to help.

"I have good days and bad days. Sometimes my hands don't work very well. I doubt if I could pick up a five-pound bag of bread flour anymore. I used to help my husband in the kitchen on Jarret's day off. We tried to make bread. Most of the time, the birds received a treat in the evening."

The men laughed.

Rowan opened the jeweler's box on the table and removed the display items in their numbered order. There were twenty pouches wrapped in fine velvet-like cloth.

The gems would not scratch each other when they moved.

The jeweler removed the first necklace, earrings, and ring from pouch number one. He took his jeweler's lens and looked at the emerald setting on the gold chain. He frowned and put down the necklace. He examined the earrings and quickly looked at the ring.

Rowan asked Jarret for a glass of water. He put the items in their bag and selected the second pouch. Again, he placed the items back in the bag. He took the water from Jarret and drank the entire glass.

After the fifteenth pouch, Mr. Edward asked for another glass of water. He loosened his tie and finished examining the rest of the pouches. The last pouch of jewelry was the largest and the most valuable. He left those items on the table and drank the second glass of water.

"Excuse me for a minute. He spoke to Fiona's lawyer, please watch the bags for me while I make a call to my office."

Horatio said, "Sure. Is there some kind of problem? The number of bags and their contents seems to be spot-on, old boy."

Fiona gave the empty juice bottle to Jarret who moved to throw the item away.

"Jarret, we have some cookies that the men might enjoy. Will you please bring in the silver dish you prepared?"

Jarret disappeared.

"I love these cookies. The bakery adds lots of butter and does deliver them free of charge. The chocolate and cherry ones are the best."

The cookies were handed to Fiona who took two and the plate was passed around. The transport guard was enjoying himself and grabbed two chocolate cookies. Jarret brought out grape and apple juice bottles. The men each took one.

Fiona was pleased her guests were enjoying the show.

The lawyer looked at Fiona and said, Mr. Edward appears to be taking a long time with his call.

Jarret saw the police cars pull up outside Ms. Kendrell's home. Rowan Edward walked back into the dining room with the lead police officer.

"Hello, ma'am."

"Hello yourself Charlie, how nice to see you? Are those kids breaking windows again in our neighborhood?"

"No, Ms. Kendrell. Tiff Sander Jeweler's man, Rowan Edward, contacted our office. The emeralds returned to you are synthetic and the diamonds are paste."

"Someone stole the emeralds and diamonds out of my necklace settings? How could they do such a thing? I'm stunned. Horatio, what do we do now?"

Horatio looked at the officer and turned to Mr. Edward.

"The collection is not my client's emerald jewelry. Every piece of expensive stone has been stolen?"

Fiona stood up.

"What?" Then she fainted. Jarret caught her and carried her with the transport guard's help. They placed the ill woman on her sofa in the living room. Fiona's eyes fluttered open.

Her lawyer sat down next to his client.

"Do you need me to contact your doctor?"

"No, I need some aspirin and water to thin my blood."

Jarret spoke, "I don't think aspirin would be good if you have fainted. I'll get the be-calm pills from your medicine cabinet."

Her butler disappeared. Her lawyer told Mr. Edward to file the report with his company. The police gave the lawyer their contact person to file documents. A police cameraman arrived to take pictures of the fake jewels and the box. The box and items were taken away as evidence.

The names of those present were recorded along with contacts for each firm.

The jeweler apologized to Fiona and told her their firm would get to the bottom of the gross mistake. The hotel would be contacted. After the jeweler, the transport company, and the police left, her lawyer talked with his client.

Jarret gave her the medicine and went to take care of the garbage.

"I don't understand."

Horatio looked at his client. "The bad news is that your jewels have been stolen. The good news is we have two estimates within the last five years that value your items at thirty-five million dollars. We don't care who their insurance company sues. You will get your money."

Fiona perked up.

"With the insurance company money, I can move to Rome near my friends. Maybe I can invest my funds? Will you still be my lawyer?"

Horatio was glad to see his client's brain rapidly firing again.

"I'll try to the best of my ability. I believe you might want to contact your friend, Sandra. You told me she mentioned the possibility of investment ideas. The

furniture and artifacts in your home would
be a nice sum of money to get you started."

"Wonderful idea. I'm bored with this
old stuff. I think the newer pieces of
furniture I see in those magazines in your
office would fit my new lifestyle nicely."

Horatio stood up to leave.

"I'll contact the Tiff Sander
Jeweler's insurance company once I have
the police report. I recommend there be no
talking with any media or anyone about the
incident. At this point, you don't know
anything about where or who could have
stolen your property."

"Good advice. My lips are sealed."

Her lawyer left the house. Jarret
came back into the room.

"How did I do, Jarret?"

He sat down next to his boss and
took her hand.

"You behaved perfectly."

Fiona was tired.

"Thank you. If you will help me, I
think the day has ended. My bones need
some rest."

Jarret helped Fiona as he did every
day. The two of them were used to the
routine.

"I never asked. Do you like Rome?"

"Absolutely, my dear."

Fiona knew her future was going to be immensely different and yet the same with Jarret close to her.

15 Insurance Investigator

Jarret let the Tiff Sander Jewelers insurance agent into the front hall and escorted him into the dining room. The round wooden table shined with a lead crystal bowl of fresh fruit on the table. A new tea cart was in the corner near the hutch. The antique hutch was full of expensive crystal and china.

"I've brought Rowan Edward with me. My name is Agent Reginald North."

Fiona introduced her lawyer, Horatio Golden.

Agent North spoke, "I find this interesting that you felt you needed your lawyer here. Our company only has a few questions about your trip before, during, and after Las Vegas."

Horatio relaxed in his chair. He let Fiona take over the show.

"Horatio Golden is a good friend of mine. I trust him completely, much like I did your representative, Jim Sloan. Jim is gone and I feel sad about his unexpected demise. I don't trust your company anymore. You've somehow lost my emeralds."

"Maam, we have the Los Angeles and Las Vegas police reports. Our company is trying to figure out at what point the jewels were switched. We obviously can't ask Jim who is now deceased. We hope to find your jewels and thieves."

"Well, talking to me isn't going to help. You should be looking at the transport company or hotel."

Horatio interrupted Fiona. "My client feels your visit is a total waste of time. She entrusted your people with literally her fortune in emeralds and diamonds. They were heirlooms from her late husband. We're glad you want to find the gems and per the signed contract have six months before you will need to pay for the loss."

The insurance agent took out his list of questions.

"You were in the house at this table when Jim Sloan examined your jewels and placed them into the velvet bags and then into our company's locked case. Who else was here?"

"Jim and one of the transport people. I think he said his name was Jantz."

"Your butler wasn't here nor your lawyer?"

"No, I trusted Jim. We did a show five years earlier with great success. The booklet your firm put together at that time showed excellent pictures of the twenty groups of my emerald and diamond collection that were to be in this show."

The insurance investigator swallowed. "Did you ever have made a matching set of paste or fake jewelry to wear instead of the emeralds?"

Fiona thought about the question.

"I don't think so. My husband was proud of the anniversary gifts he gave me. In those days, women could wear their good jewelry without fear of being robbed. My jewels were probably stolen in broad daylight right in front of your company."

"Ms. Kendrell, your jewels weren't just good jewelry. They were rare and exceptional in color and quality. I might mention Jim's praise about the stones. He said they were *priceless*."

Horatio smiled and wrote some notes in his black book.

The insurance agent looked at Rowan.

"Per Mr. Edward, the fakes were also exceptionally designed."

"And very beautiful," quipped Rowan.

"Whoever made the fakes is an exceptional craftsman. However, there was no maker's mark anywhere on the stones or settings. Our company finds this lack very unusual."

Horatio looked up, "The lack of markings wasn't unusual for the thieves. They probably were ecstatic with the fakes."

Fiona was surprised by her lawyer.

"Now, Horatio, that was a terrible thing to say."

The insurance agent asked Fiona if she met any of her friends at the show or if anyone helped her.

Fiona looked at her lawyer. He nodded.

"My travel companion and hairdresser, Candy Evans, went with me. Jarret went on vacation to be with his son. I did meet a good friend of mine, Sandra Delray. We ate appetizers together in the hotel."

"Have those two people seen your emeralds?"

Fiona carefully replied. "Candy has not. Sandra dated my nephew, Demonte Duran for four years. During that time, she saw some of the emeralds when I wore them to charity events, garden and rose meetings, plays, and symphonies. But then lots of people saw my jewels up close and personal."

Reginald North frowned. He wrote some notes down. "Let's continue the path of the jewels. Jim handed the case to the transport person. In other words, he never left this room before the case was taken away from your property by the transport company?"

"We did have tea while we waited for the transport vehicle and guards. Jim filled the silver teapot for me after he put the jewels in the case. He was in the kitchen a couple of minutes."

The insurance agent asked the next disturbing question, "Did you open the case and take out the jewels while Jim was busy?"

Horatio stood up.

"Sit down, Horatio. Mr. North, I'm an old woman who has lived a very rich life. My hands and strength aren't as good as they used to be. However, my brain is still intact. Anyway, most of the time, the cylinders are firing. There are days when I am out of sorts. Maybe your company needs a different investigator if you must accuse an old woman. There would be no reason for me to steal my own jewels. I already own them. The large case of jewels would have been too heavy for me to lift and it would take too long to open the compartments to remove the jewels."

Reginald sighed and flipped his page over.

"The transport people put the case in a locked bin on their truck. They drove directly to the hotel without any stops. The case was delivered to the High Tower Plaza Hotel security desk where the jewels were locked in their guest vault area. Your jewels remained in the vault until Sunday. The decision to leave them in the vault was made after there was a water leak next to the showroom. The section of your show was postponed until Monday noon. The jewels were removed from the case Monday morning and put inside the twenty display cases and those cases were locked."

"I believe that was the chain of events. I never saw my emeralds again after they were taken from my home. I flew back to Los Angeles on Saturday after the scheduled luncheon. My escort and hairdresser went with me."

"Jim Sloan had a heart attack before the show opened. The display cases were relocked, and three security guards stayed to guard the doors. Jim died the next day and Jim's assistant later repacked the jewels when the show was canceled. The jewels were in their pouches inside the case. A different transport company arrived and took the jewels. They drove directly here with no stops."

Horatio spoke, "I was here when the transport company arrived to return the jewels as was Fiona and Jarret, her butler. We saw Rowan Edward unpack the case. The returned emeralds and diamonds were fake. End of story."

Reginald scratched his head. "Why were you here when the jewels returned, Mr. Golden? Were you expecting trouble?"

Fiona's eyes rolled upwards to the ceiling.

"Jim was the man I trusted. I didn't know this Rowan person from your firm or which transport was chosen to bring my emerald and diamonds back to me. The transport company for the return wasn't listed in the contract. My lawyer caught the omission."

Reginald flipped his notebook shut.

"My company will continue with the investigation. We will review the transport people and the hotel plus their procedures in handling the jewels. Ms. Kendrell, thank you for your time."

He turned to leave.

"Oh, one more question. There's no tablecloth on the table. The guard with the first transport mentioned a long tablecloth."

Fiona said, "We use the tablecloth when we serve tea."

Mr. North looked at the tea cart with the expensive silver tea service in the corner. The pot was too small to hide the jewels and the cart contained open shelving. The crystal in the china hutch was a little dusty and hadn't been moved. The bottom of the hutch was open. There was no place to really hide the jewels.

"Goodbye, Mr. Golden. I'm sure we will be talking in the future."

"Yes, I expect we will," said Horatio.

After they left, Fiona's lawyer mentioned the tea cart in the corner was new.

"Oh, yes, the old one developed a wheel problem. Jarret put the item in the garage. The wood is rose mahogany and the wood is hard to buy plus we'll need a carpenter to hand carve another wheel."

"I always liked that cart. Wasn't there a wood tray that popped up a level to the table?"

"Yes, the wood tray is inlaid with ivory."

The lawyer nodded.

"You should get the cart repaired. I'm sure the piece is very valuable."

Fiona smiled, "Indeed. I've been told it could be worth up to a million dollars due to the elephant ivory. The knobs are ivory and gold."

"Good heavens."

Fiona laughed.

"Thank you for not mentioning the cart. Otherwise, I think Agent Reginald North would have put me in the hoosegow."

"Fiona, we might both end up in prison yet. I figure we have twenty more years to get into trouble."

The two watched as Jarret put the tablecloth on the wood table and removed the fruit bowl. The filled silver teapot was placed on top of the cart and the cups were assembled.

"Tea, Horatio?"

"I thought you would never ask."

"There's a rose show in Pasadena soon and I was wondering if you and your wife would like to attend with me."

Horatio took a sip of the hot tea.

"I'm sure she would like to go. Let me get back to you."

16 Sandra Flies Home

Three months passed since the news media printed the story in Las Vegas about the Green Emerald Heist. The story noted that the jeweler's emeralds were not stolen, only Ms. Kendrell's emeralds and diamond jewelry. The newspaper wondered where the blame should be laid. They were stumped by the mystery as were the police.

Sandra flew to Los Angeles and met with Fiona at her favorite restaurant in Oceanside. Jarret would return in two hours for his boss. After they ordered a seafood bowl of soup, Sandra gladly gave her friend some recommendations to consider.

"Why not leave Demonte this house in California in your will. This will please him and Petrissa. You might want to invest in some properties that my women's club wants to purchase here and abroad.

"Both ideas sound interesting. Tell me more."

Sandra continued.

"We pool some of our money for targeted houses that need upgrades. My people coordinate the rebuild contractors and material. Each person's percentage will be calculated from the amount they invested when the property is sold. There's money to be made and we have the right combination of talent to succeed."

"Once the money from the insurance arrives, I won't need to invest," said Fiona.

Sandra rolled this argument around in her prior planning.

"Yes, this is very true. However, you could live in some of the properties when they get finished until you find one that you really like. You would be helping women to succeed. Your past charities have helped many women."

"I should do something more with my life. I've met most of your group. The only one that I haven't met is Darcy."

"Darcy told me she would come to see you. She'd like to take some pictures of your roses and if you don't mind, take a few cuttings. Her garden is spectacular."

"I wonder if I can take some cuttings of my flowers with me when I move?"

Sandra shook her head.

"The airlines probably won't allow plants but maybe you can ship some. I'll ask Darcy to check with various shippers."

"My lawyer should help with the law part of my investments."

Sandra looked excitedly at her friend.

"Of course, my answer is yes. I'm quite fond of you. I want to join your club on a more permanent basis."

Sandra hugged Fiona.

"Now, the will would need to be changed, to accommodate us for the investments in case of your demise. The rest of your money could be left to friends, art galleries, etc. after you have passed away."

Fiona burst out laughing.

"This will leave Demonte outside of our women's party."

"Exactly."

"He will be mad and come after you."

"I'm not afraid."

Sandra sat back in her chair and waited. Fiona looked at the ocean. The seagulls were flying and dipping into the water. Fiona wanted to feel carefree again. She remembered the concert in London. Sandra's energy brought life into her soul.

Sandra handed this new opportunity for change to Fiona on a silver platter. The strings were to help and support her friends. Fiona wondered if Sandra would want her tea service when she was gone. A new will would need to be craftily drawn up, so her word was preserved. She thought about the gift route. Horatio would guide Fiona with her final wishes.

"What is the name of your women's companies so that I can pass the information to my lawyer?"

Sandra handed her the list of the company names with PO Boxes and addresses. The bank and account numbers were included with each address.

"I'm definitely into the investor plan. I think being a real estate investor would brighten my day. Living in different places sounds exciting. How wonderful to be able to enjoy a new life in Rome!"

Sandra stood to go. She held Fiona's hand.

"I would take the bronzes and paintings with me."

Fiona smiled evilly.

"But, of course, I'll order some new vases I saw at an art show. They would look perfect for a rental."

Fiona rose when she saw Jarret. He helped his boss to the vehicle parked at the curb. Sandra waved her friend goodbye.

17 Stop in Las Vegas

The airplane landed at the Las Vegas Airport and Sandra took the shuttle to the Splendor and Devon Casino. She arrived at nine o'clock in the evening. She left her luggage with the guest's security desk. Not checking in, she walked through the lobby and went to the set of elevators on the first floor.

Sandra debated about calling Craig. At the last minute, she changed her mind. After her stop in Vegas, she would fly to Phoenix to get Henri. Then, she would return to Rome.

There was a mob of people waiting to get on the elevators. Sandra stepped aside next to a tall plant. The closest elevator opened, and she saw Craig Connor step out. He turned to take the hand of a gorgeous young dark-haired woman. He put his arms around her and pulled her close. Craig stopped to kiss the woman.

Sandra was pushed by the throng onto the elevator. She stepped inside and didn't punch any buttons. The other patrons selected their floors. At the top, she stepped out and went to the restaurant.

The waiter brought her a menu. She needed to eat something.

"French Salad and coffee with cream."

The waiter quickly brought her the items. She needed time to think. The salad was good despite her inner turmoil. The cream was poured into the steaming coffee.

"I'm glad that I didn't make room reservations."

Her plan to visit Craig backfired.

"I've not been smart. The club women have agreed to no serious relationships. Here I am wanting more. I won't do this move again."

She called the number for the High Tower Plaza Hotel. They did have a room for her. She booked the room and called the airline to change her return reservation for a flight in the morning.

The waiter asked if she needed anything.

"No, I have all I need for the moment. Thank you for asking."

The waiter showed her the check and she handed over her credit card. When he returned the card, she left the restaurant and rode the elevator. Retrieving her luggage, she walked out of Craig's hotel. She went across the street.

Once in her room, she called Danielle.

Danielle answered and knew things went badly.

"Fiona wasn't feeling well?"

"No, Fiona is fine. She is very good, indeed. I made a stop in Las Vegas."

Danielle did a little dance.

"I'm glad. How's the trip going while at the Vegas hotel?"

Sandra stopped for a minute.

"Let's say the two people who got off the elevator were uninspiring. No one saw me. I went across the street."

"Ouch. I see the visual picture flashing across my brain. You must be flying sooner than expected to Phoenix to get Henri?"

"Yes, tomorrow."

"I'll see you when you get back to Rome."

Sandra hung up the call. In the morning she boarded her flight.

Kevin Meadow, the security person at the Splendor and Devon Casino, poured himself a cup of coffee. His day off was yesterday. The new security person needed to be monitored for another month. Craig Connor wanted his hotel to run smoothly. Mr. Connor was big into training his employees properly.

Kevin reviewed the tapes from the previous day. He saw the blond woman walk

through the front lobby toward their
elevators. He spilled his coffee in trying to
reach for the halt button on the film. He
enlarged the frame while wiping the coffee.

He stopped moving.

"It's her."

Kevin put his hand over his mouth.
He reviewed the other cameras and saw her
exit the elevator and go into the restaurant.
He watched as she came out of the
restaurant and went to the elevator.
Switching quickly to the lobby, he saw her
exit their hotel. Kevin zoomed the door.

"She ate here and went across the
street. Nobody eats here and walks across
the street. They usually stay."

He chewed on his knuckles. Kevin
called the prior day's guard on the landline.

"Timmy, did Mr. Connor talk with
you yesterday about any visitor that stopped
by our hotel around nine in the evening?"

Timmy hadn't talked with Mr.
Connor because the man was on a date.

"No," said Timmy.

Kevin grimaced his face. Timmy was
not full of information this morning.

"Mr. Connor *did not* talk to you
yesterday? Please explain his reasons."

"He was busy."

Kevin drum-rolled his fingers on the keyboard. The words he typed were, *kill, kill, kill.*

"Now, Timmy, listen very carefully. Mr. Connor was busy yesterday. He was busy with a person is my guess. This person must have been our guest."

"I don't know if she was a guest."

Kevin banged his head on the table.

"We've isolated the facts. Mr. Connor was with a female. Mr. Connor was with whom?"

"You know."

Kevin's temper flared. He yelled on the phone.

"Her name!"

Timmy took the phone away from his ear.

"The Tamara person. I can't remember her last name. I think you broke my eardrum."

Kevin wanted to box more than Timmy's ears. He sat back and hung up on Timmy. He re-scrolled through the elevator cameras until he found the couple entering a down elevator. He looked at the time stamp.

"I'm dead."

The door opened behind Kevin and a well-dressed Craig Connor entered the security room of his hotel.

"Morning, Kevin, you look beat. Your vacation was supposed to be relaxing. I thought your family was going to the new wave pool."

"I should have drowned myself."

Craig looked at his employee and saw the extra monitor of him and his date. Then he saw the screen of Sandra entering the hotel. He looked at the timestamps.

Craig sat down in a chair.

"Oh, no. She didn't call or answer for three months and she magically arrives at my hotel."

Kevin went to get them both a cup of coffee.

Craig was going through the same screens Kevin previously watched. Craig stopped the restaurant door screen. Punching the restaurant number, he talked to the maître d'.

"She ate here. There was no problem with her salad and coffee."

Setting the coffee cups down, the security guard waited.

"Ms. Delray saw me exit the elevator with my date."

Kevin was going to say that they couldn't be sure about whether Ms. Delray saw the couple, but he knew that would be wrong.

"Nobody eats here and walks across the street. They usually stay."

"There was no reason for her to stay after I exited from the first-floor elevator with my date in tow."

Kevin pondered.

"Maybe flowers would work with expensive champagne on ice. We have two bottles of the stuff in case of an emergency. I would consider this scene an emergency."

"She's worth more than those two bottles of champagne."

"You're right. A roomful of flowers thrown in might help. My wife likes flowers when she is mad. Or you could always transfer to the nearest hotel where she is currently living."

Craig shook his head.

"Your wife gets mad?"

Kevin snorted, "All women get mad. My wife is better at recovery than most."

Craig could visualize a whole suite-full of flowers dumped right back at his doorstep. Sandra might be the type to throw things.

"Elephants don't forget."

Kevin reconsidered.

"Ms. Delray might take a year to calm down."

"I think you are absolutely correct."

Craig was to blame for his mess. However, Sandra's name and picture were noted in the guest's arrival book as a top priority guest for their hotel. The hotel protocol wasn't followed. The manager of the hotel should have been notified.

Craig said one word, "Timmy?"

Kevin was responsible for the employee.

"He wasn't paying attention."

Craig drank his coffee down and tossed the cup in the garbage.

"Two weeks' notice."

Kevin looked crestfallen.

Craig caught himself, "If he doesn't perform better in two weeks, we need to let Timmy go. You would have caught her immediately. She walks differently than most women."

"Confidence. She is smooth like a model walking an expensive runway. Yes, the visual would have been immediate. By the way, thank you for the compliment, sir."

Craig left the room to go to his penthouse and make a call. The person on the other end of the call didn't answer. He left Sandra a message and waited. After an hour, he returned to his duties as a hotel manager. He knew Sandra was gone for good. There would be no return call and he didn't know where she lived in Rome.

Craig looked at the website for their Rome hotel. He made a call to the manager. There were no guests by her name at their hotel.

"Do me a favor. If she ever checks into the hotel, please contact me immediately with an urgent message."

"I will do as you have asked, Mr. Connor. You can always plan a visit to our hotel in the future. I can personally give you a tour if I'm on duty."

"Call me Craig. I might do that very thing. Seeing how our other hotels operate is always educational."

"Arrivederci, Craig."

18 Insurance Report

Reginald North met with his
superiors. The six-month investigation
period was over on Ms. Kendrell's claim for
thirty-five million dollars.

The head of the board took charge of
the meeting.

"We've read the brief and looked at
the massive reports. How could this have
happened to our company? We've never had
a problem of this magnitude."

"Those are all the facts that I could
find, sir."

"Perhaps we should have hired an
outside investigative firm rather than you,
Mr. North."

Reginald winced. An old lady told
him the same thing over five months ago.

One of the board members asked a
question.

"The police believe the thieves might
have entered the hotel via the sewer system
when there was a food fair happening. They
found a ladder and some gloves in the
sewer. There are doors in the cement to both
hotels. The Splendor and Devon Casino
door was unlocked. Who unlocked the door?

I don't understand why there was a door to the hotel from the sewer system."

"In the old days, they built the structures that way. The door was to allow escape in case of fire in the sewer. The door keys were carried by a head worker. None of those people unlocked this door recently."

The board member shook his head, "Maybe they forgot. Well, gentlemen, then do we sue the city?"

"We can't. The doors supposedly were given to the hotel in some agreement. The lock is on the sewer side. Both hotels would fight about who owned the lock. There was a second door at the show hotel which showed marks that the door was pried open."

"I'm confused."

"The underground door by the Splendor and Devon Casino was unlocked. We don't think the thieves used their door. The underground door by the High Tower Plaza shows some marks. The hotel commented the marks could have been there for some time. There were no metal filings on the floor. Their assumption was their door wasn't part of this crime."

The board member asked, "Fingerprints?"

"None."

Reginald clicked on his presentation
and pulled up a copy of the city document.
Then he moved past a few other screens.

"The folding ladder was found close
to the heat ducts in the High Tower Plaza.
The heat duct runs past the security room
where the locked guest valuables are kept."

The board man objected.

"There must be cement blocking the
heat ducts from the security room
compartments where the guest valuables are
stored?"

Reginald pushed the button on his
presentation to show the compartments were
wood at the top. He showed the dimension
of the wood which was a half an inch.

"So, none of the people in the
building heard the perps use a saw to cut the
wood?"

Reginald sighed. He flipped to
another screen. The screen showed the
outside of the heat vent and small boards
nailed to the half-inch thick wood.

"All the thieves needed were a good
hammer to pry the nails to access the case of
jewels which contained Ms. Kendrell's
emeralds and diamonds. They probably had
lots of time to do the exchange. Thank
goodness our jewels were secure."

Reginald paused the presentation.

"But we aren't sure this is exactly what happened, and the hotel is fighting us on this issue. The hotel blames the transport company and us. There are also fake jewels. The police have no idea where they came from or when they entered the theft incident. They assumed a switch happened. The thieves could have set up a dummy run."

The head of the board said, "Idiots. The ladder and gloves could have been down in the sewer for years. We're the sitting ducks in this scenario. The timing was key here. The thieves were way ahead of everybody. We haven't heard of the jewels being sold in the underground nor any private investor citing's. The thieves are smart. They are waiting. Therefore, gentlemen, we must pay money to Ms. Fiona Kendrell. Horatio Golden, her lawyer, has already contacted us about our oversight in issuing the wire transfer. We will have to fight our battle with the hotel and transport company alone. I doubt we will get a resolution in our favor."

The other board member became angry and argued.

"I believe the police. Someone must have seen the thieves. Didn't we talk to the food trucks at the fair? Surely, someone saw people carrying a ladder and a box or large bag. The twenty bags of jewelry were heavy."

Reginald answered. "We interviewed the food truck owners and examined the trucks. There was nothing. Yes, they saw people with all sorts of equipment, ladders, dollies, boxes, etc. They have ladders on their trucks that do come off and folding ladders like the one the police found. As far as unusual, heck, the whole state of Nevada is strange. People dress up, wear gold and purple hair, leather boots, tattoos, and smoke drugs up their noses and who-knows-where else. The gloves could have been left behind by a worker. A rat might have carried the glove to its resting place."

The board member couldn't believe their firm was at a dead end.

"In other words, our brochure from five years ago gave some big rat the idea to create perfect fakes and these dirty thieving rats waited for another show to take a run and dump."

Reginald turned off his computer and sat down.

"It certainly looks that way."

"Well, who approached Ms. Kendrell about this show?"

The head member said, "Jim Sloan thought another show would be a good idea."

"Nuts!"

All the board members sat in silence.

Reginald looked at the head member. He spoke.

"Accounting will issue the wire tomorrow after we have moved some funds."

Reginald packed his computer in his briefcase.

"I'll contact Fiona's lawyer. I'm sure he will be elated."

19 Rome Fixer-Upper

Sandra and Danielle walked
through the rooms. The furniture finally
arrived. Danielle showed the delivery
persons where the L-shaped sofa and coffee
table were to be placed in the room. The
other workers were installing a murphy-bed
in the only bedroom.

This renovation house was tiny with
approximately eight hundred and twenty feet
of livable space. There was a smaller room
off the back of the single car garage and
balcony.

"I don't know. We should probably
have ditched the garage idea and gone for a
master bedroom."

Sandra had nixed the idea. "A master
bedroom would require large closets and a
second bath. We couldn't afford the extra
charge on this one. We need a bigger home
to splurge. We can do the luxurious master
next time."

Danielle looked over the hill and the
water below.

"I love this view. People will pay for
the fresh air and image. I'm so glad we don't
have to sleep in those ugly cots anymore."

Sandra smiled.

126

"I like the idea of a running shower. I'm tired of lugging and heating my water in a plastic tub."

Danielle was happy. They found jobs quickly as waiters and decided against staying at a hotel.

"Fiona liked the pictures of this cottage that I sent. She and Jarret are thinking about this one for living arrangements. She prefers our first choice for the second house rebuild and has agreed to fund four million on the next one."

Danielle screamed with delight.

"Oh, thank you, thank you. With our two million off this place, we can splurge."

Sandra knew things were moving along. She was waiting for a reply from their realtor on their second prospective purchase.

A year passed since the emerald heist. The other women in their group were working on their rebuilds. Fiona received her check for the theft of her jewels from the Tiff Sander Jeweler's insurance company and would be moving to Rome shortly.

Sandra was happy. Henri was in his cage tweeting loudly. She saw him eating his sunflower seeds.

"We might want to have Henri stay at the veterinary place for a week while we take a nice vacation. I think we have earned the right to relax. Where would you like to stay?"

Danielle thought about a hotel that was close to their first rebuild and the restaurant was excellent. She was tired of eating cheap pasta.

"I choose the hotel called the Splendor and Devon Casino."

Sandra looked at Danielle in surprise.

"The hotel in Rome is usually booked months in advance."

"We can at least try."

Sandra thought about Craig Connor. He wouldn't be at this location. She would be safe from his attentions. Besides, he already kept a girlfriend on the side. She wondered how many other women he flirted with that came through his hotel.

"I'll call tomorrow."

Danielle handed her the cell phone.

"Please!"

"This is crazy."

Danielle's eyes blinked rapidly.

"We already know those facts. Dial!"

Sandra made the call. The reservation clerk looked at the time period she mentioned which was a month away. The clerk asked if she could call her back.

"There might be a cancellation the manager knows about. They have the most recent stuff on their system."

Sandra gave her the phone number.

"See, there isn't anything available."

Danielle frowned and took an apple out of the wooden bowl. Sandra did the same. Both women pulled out their computers to check their mail.

Sandra's phone rang. Danielle brightened. Sandra frowned and answered the call.

The hotel clerk told her about the rooms available. The queen bed in the single bedroom would be adequate for their needs for a week. The room space was in the corner and there was a partial view of the ocean. The plus side was the kitchenette and fireplace. The hotel clerk gave Sandra the price. The manager of the hotel was standing by the hotel clerk listening to the call.

"Is there any way we could get a reduced price?"

The manager nodded.

"This room comes with a two-hundred-dollar gift certificate at any of our restaurants."

Sandra gave the information to Danielle. Daniele was quietly clapping her hands.

"We'll take the room."

Sandra finished the hotel booking transaction. The two women sunk into their newly purchased couch with happiness at the thought of a week of playtime.

The manager of the hotel went to his office to contact an interested party. He was going to send a note and decided a phone call would be a better method of communication.

A more luxurious suite was booked for a manager of their hotel chain from the United States.

20 Rome Holiday

Danielle slipped into the pool water at the Splendor and Devon Casino in Rome. Sandra quickly joined her.

"Hey, don't splash," said Danielle. Sandra scooped up some water and heaved the wet flow toward Danielle. She screamed and went after Sandra. After thoroughly dunking her, both women swam together for a while.

A man near the outside pool bar sat watching the two women play. He waited until they came out of the pool, dried themselves, and laid back in their lounge chairs to catch some sun.

He strolled toward the blonde in the yellow one-piece swimsuit. She looked like her modeling photos. Fiona told him Sandra modeled her way through college.

He sat down in the lounge next to Sandra and waited for the barman to bring the two women refreshments. Danielle turned over first and saw Craig. She picked up her drink and saluted with the glass.

Danielle bent down and whispered to Sandra.

"Your dinosaur is here."

Sandra slowly turned over. His eyes appreciatively looked at her thin frame.

*"You look amazingly wet and
supremely healthy."*

"Do I know you?"

Sandra took a sip of her drink.

"Coconut and a touch of pineapple,
how nice! I was right. I don't know you.
Goodbye."

Craig frowned.

"I suppose a roomful of flowers and
very expensive champagne aren't going to
work either."

"You are correct."

Now Craig was at a loss. He kept
looking at Sandra. He had all day. She knew
he wasn't going away.

"What is the name of the
champagne?"

He told her the name and the year.

"How expensive?"

"A thousand dollars a bottle."

Sandra put her drink down on the
small table, closed her eyes, and said, "I'll
think about the champagne."

Craig waited five minutes. She could
feel him still staring at her and heard the ice
swirling in his glass. She opened her eyes
and sat up.

"I went to your hotel expecting to
visit a friend."

"I know. The security cameras caught your image. The protocol wasn't followed."

She looked at him and then watched some children playing in the pool.

"I'm on a protocol list. How wonderful!"

Craig moved in his chair. "The police came to my hotel in Las Vegas and asked me if there was anyone that I knew who looked suspicious. You see, an elderly lady's emerald and diamond jewelry were stolen at a hotel across the street. Imagine my surprise to hear the elderly woman's name. You were with Fiona Kendrell."

Sandra took her beach top and slipped her hands through the sleeves.

"Fiona is a dear friend of mine. I've known her for some time. She was upset about the loss of her emeralds."

"Did you steal Fiona's emeralds?"

Sandra's eyes turned dark.

"No. Now if you will excuse me, I need to find a much better company for conversation."

Craig watched her stomp away as fast as she could go in bare feet.

"Nice job, Craig, my boy. You just blew your last chance at happiness."

It was a good thing he ordered two bottles of expensive champagne. Craig stopped by the flower shop and selected a bouquet of yellow roses. He didn't even know what type of flowers she liked. He gave the florist his order for delivery.

Walking to Danielle and Sandra's hotel room door, he lightly knocked. Danielle opened the door.

"She won't talk to you because you were rude."

Craig handed Danielle one of the expensive bottles.

"Wow, I've heard of this brand. You are smooth. You brought two glasses and flowers."

Danielle stepped aside and let Craig into their room. She pointed toward the bedroom. He walked over, opened the door, stepped inside, and shut the door.

Danielle put her champagne in the refrigerator, grabbed her purse, and left the two people alone.

Sandra was tying the front of her sundress when she saw him.

"You forgot to tell me whether we were going to drink champagne."

"Persistent, aren't we? My answer is no."

"I'm always persistent when someone is important. I know what I like."

"There's the girlfriend and how many others in your little world?"

Craig knew she would circle back to the sore subject. He remembered the elephant theory.

"Gone. She was the only one besides you. We didn't get very far."

She slammed her suitcase shut.

Craig ignored her, placed the flowers on the dresser, and opened the champagne. He poured her a glass and himself a glass. Walking toward Sandra, he handed her the glass.

Slowly she took the glass and took a drink. He clinked her glass and took a sip.

"To us!"

Sandra blinked. The champagne was awesome. She was confused by the statement. They weren't a couple.

He put the two glasses down on the wood. Stepping close, he kissed her and whispered, "I'm in love with you from your hair to your toes."

Sandra finally understood why he continued to follow her. There was no need to worry. Her girl power was the attraction. Craig was feeling the same desires she felt in Las Vegas when Sandra dropped her guard.

"Craig Connor, you want to make out with me after one kiss?"

"Yes, ma'am. I think we should drink champagne and go to dinner first. There are more flowers in my hotel room."

"A whole suite full?"

"Absolutely, every color of the rainbow because I didn't know which color to pick."

"Yellow or gold is my favorite color and definitely emerald green."

Craig started laughing.

"You are bad."

"I've decided to change my ways," said Sandra.

"You're lying. I saw you open your mouth. People usually blink when they lie. You don't blink."

Sandra batted her eyes at him and opened her mouth. He kissed her some more and she responded in kind.

Craig held her, "That kiss was worth the wait."

"There are many more kisses to follow. You might have to earn them. Maybe we should wait until tomorrow."

"No."

"No?"

"You heard me."

Sandra smiled. She liked teasing Craig. He pulled her closer.

The champagne warmed before they left the room to go to dinner.

Danielle saw them later exiting the building to go to the hotel's more extravagant restaurant next door near the ocean.

"Finally, I can get back into my room." She went to the refrigerator and saw the opened champagne bottle. She touched the glass.

"I probably shouldn't put ice cubes with this champagne. I'll wait."

Danielle changed her clothes. Seeing the flowers, she put them in a decorative vase. She went with some friends to dinner. When she arrived back at her hotel room, the open bottle was missing. There was a note written in Sandra's hand in the spot where the bottle previously rested on the shelf.

"Fat chance I'm leaving this behind. Drink your own bottle. I'm taking Craig to the rebuilt house tomorrow. We'll be back in the evening at about seven. Save tomorrow night. Craig is buying."

Danielle was glad they were trying to include her. She was happy for her friend. Danielle remembered Las Vegas.

"The sap liked Sandra even in the States."

21 Time with Craig

Danielle drove to the finished
rebuild house which they called the cottage.
Craig walked through the kitchen and tiny
living room. He whistled with praise.

"The view of the ocean is stunning."
He wandered into the bedroom and saw the
murphy bed and comfortable chairs. There
was a partial view of the ocean from the
bedroom window. He noted the nice shower
and bath area.

"We put in a small garage and a
deck. There are steps that were repaired.
You can walk down to the beach and take a
short walk at low tide."

Craig took her hand.

"Let's go to the beach."

They maneuvered the steps and
walked the short distance to an outcropping
of rocks.

"I see the tide has turned. We should
go back."

By the time they arrived at the
staircase, the waves were splashing their
feet. When they reached the top deck, the
two young lovers removed their sneakers.
They sat on the newly arranged outside
chairs and listened to the surf.

"Who is Henri? Should I be jealous? I forgot to ask if there is a boyfriend."

Sandra smiled. "He's my bird. We can stop by the veterinarian's place on our way back to the hotel. No is my answer to the boyfriend question."

"Good."

"How did you know about Henri?"

Craig looked guilty.

"Aah, yes, the security camera at the Las Vegas hotel."

"I enjoyed last night," said Craig.

"I did, too. There's been no one for some time. I forgot how nice being with someone feels."

He touched her hand and held it. The two lovers were currently calm. They both knew something was happening between them.

"How long do you plan on staying in Rome?"

Sandra looked at Craig. "I'd like to finish the second rebuild and then I'll look at my next steps. For now, I haven't made any further plans."

Craig scooted his chair closer.

"I know we have the rest of this week together. Then I leave on Saturday. I will have a hard time not seeing you for six months."

"I know. I've thought about your leaving. I can fly to Las Vegas on occasion."

"I can also fly here. I'm probably going to have to make the timing to match when I can get away from my job."

Sandra thought about what he told her.

"I'm okay with waiting for you. I haven't found anyone else interesting enough to date."

Craig was delighted. She wanted to also see where their relationship was headed.

"There's no old boyfriends in the closet waiting for you to return?"

She hit him in the arm. "You're the one who has hidden women."

"Not anymore. Seriously, should I be on the lookout for a secret admirer?"

A cloud crossed Sandra's face. She picked up her tennis shoes and went inside. Craig followed. She handed him a cold bottle of water.

"I should tell you about Demonte Duran. He is Fiona Kendrell's nephew. We dated four years and broke off. He's married now."

Craig scowled. "I think I saw his name on occasion. He runs around with the celebrities."

"Yes. He's been traveling on a South American tour. Now I believe they are touring Europe on Fiona's money."

"Do you think he knows about the missing emeralds?"

Sandra drank some of her water.

"No, I don't think so. Otherwise, he would be in her face looking for another handout. He probably also doesn't know she's selling her furniture and artifacts and has plans on living in Rome."

"This Demonte guy could give Fiona trouble. What about you when he finds out she's one of your investors?"

"Fiona can handle her nephew. I don't need to have any business with him anymore."

Craig bent down and kissed her neck. "Do you want to play poker?"

She looked at his eyes. He was teasing her.

"If we play poker, I'll win."

He kissed her again. "I know."

"What's the pot? Money?"

"No, there's something much more valuable."

Sandra hesitated.

"I give."

"I want you to win. The pot is me."

She laughed.

141

"Why waste all that time with the cards? All you have to say is that I won."

Craig said, "You won."

She took his hand and guided him toward the tiny bedroom.

After a tumultuous week of vacation and play, Sandra kissed him goodbye at the gate to his airplane. She watched him walk to the ramp and the ticket agent. He turned and waved one last time.

Driving back to the veterinarian, Sandra picked up Henri and went back to the cottage. She opened the kitchen door and saw Danielle putting tape on another box.

Henri's cage was placed on the small island and she took his cover off. Getting the bird water and more food, she petted him and reclosed the cage door. The bird started making happy noises.

"I'm tired. I missed a week's worth of sleep."

Danielle stopped reading her magazine.

"Was the lack of sleep worth it?"

Sandra smiled, "Way beyond my expectations."

"Mr. Connor will be returning to Rome in the future? You'll need to inform the others."

"I certainly hope he will. I'll call Candy. She can spread the news."

Sandra answered her phone and listened to Fiona. She whispered to Danielle, "Demonte is home in Los Angeles."

22 Run-in with Mr. North

Craig was doing rounds of the floors of the Splendor and Devon Casino in Las Vegas when a familiar man approached him. Three weeks passed since his trip to Rome.

"Mr. Reginald North, you are walking in our hotel. Is there some reason for this unannounced visit?"

"My company would like me to continue with our search for some answers regarding the Fiona Kendrell jewel mishap."

"Really. I thought the Tiff Sander Jewelers have paid the insurance claim?"

"We have, but the investigation is ongoing. We are interested in persons who may have stayed at your hotel that knew Ms. Kendrell. Mostly, we are interested in a year before the theft and six months afterward. There's one name that jumps out."

"Do I know the person in question?"

"Yes, we were told you visited Rome to see her."

Craig blinked. "Sandra Delray?"

"Yes, and anyone connected with her."

"Our company has privacy laws. I can't divulge any information to you unless you have an order from the court."

Mr. North handed him the required document.

"Come with me," said Craig.

They went inside his security office. He handed a piece of paper to Kevin Meadow to pull the dates Ms. Delray stayed at their hotel and the names and dates of any of her guests.

After fifteen minutes, Kevin handed his boss the list. The hotel lawyer joined the meeting in Mr. Connor's office. The hotel lawyer reviewed the documents. He pulled out additional documents for Mr. North to sign as a receipt. Craig made a copy for the hotel's files and for their lawyer.

"Thank you for your time, gentlemen."

Mr. North exited Mr. Connor's office and left the hotel grounds.

Craig looked at his hotel's lawyer.

"I've spent a week in Rome at our hotel there with Ms. Delray. We are in a relationship."

The lawyer took out his pen and wrote down the information.

"At this point, if Mr. North again enters the hotel unannounced, you kindly inform him to contact me directly. You will not talk to the man about any of our past hotel clients or our future hotel clients. You might want to call your own lawyer to apprise him of the situation."

"The insurance company is upset about losing a large sum of money. They need to blame someone."

The lawyer looked at Craig.

"You are correct on that score."

The hotel lawyer left the building.

Craig sat in his office drumming the ink pen on the desk. He went to his penthouse and made the call to his lawyer. Next, he contacted Sandra.

"Hi, sweetheart, I'm glad you picked up your phone. Let's get married."

Sandra was speechless.

"I need a moment."

Craig waited.

"I want a three-carat emerald cut diamond, top-grade, in white gold in size six and a half."

Sandra waited. She was kidding him.

"Done. I need a week to make my arrangements. How about you?"

Now she was really puzzled. He wasn't making any logical sense. She knew something was wrong. Sandra decided to play along.

"We might have a problem. I'm working with the pool people. They will take longer than a week."

"Push them back."

Sandra wondered if Craig was drunk. He usually only drank one or two glasses of wine or champagne at the most.

"Time is money," said Sandra.

"Do you love me?"

She looked at her cell phone as if there was a genie inside reading her mind. They hadn't talked about love or trust or her secrets. She hid many things from him.

"Secretly, yes, I do."

Craig couldn't help but smile.

"I'll call you when my plans are firm. I miss you."

"I miss you, too."

Craig disconnected the call. He went online and moved some money. Next, he called his favorite jeweler. He called his manager to get the time off and left the office to get the ring. He stopped at his administrator's office to tell her to make airline, hotel, and rental car arrangements.

23 Rome Decision

Craig drove to the second rebuild home. Danielle and Sandra were waiting for him. Craig immediately kissed Sandra and smiled. Danielle pressed Craig's arm and exited the home. She would find out later what was wrong.

Craig sat his briefcase and luggage down. She brought him a hot cup of coffee and they went into the kitchen. He told her about the ongoing investigation between the Tiff Sander Jewelers Insurance Company and the police.

Sandra played with her cup of tea twirling the slice of lemon.

"I've talked to my lawyer. He told me the only way to stop me from testifying would be to marry you. I thought about marriage and the idea sounds like fun."

Sandra looked at Craig as if he lost his marbles.

"This is too soon. We barely know each other. I have secrets. You probably have secrets."

"No, I'm the open book. You're the one with the secret club."

"You're speculating about my friends."

"I don't think so. You know the plumber we hired to change out our water heater. They removed the wallboard. My understanding is a room resides below that room. The room connects through a door to the sewer line. The sewer line runs across the street to the High Tower Plaza Hotel where there's another door that accesses their building. If I can figure out something this complicated, so can Mr. North."

"I didn't steal the emeralds and diamonds. I've told you before. I doubt Darcy knows about sewers and rooms. She's also a heavy-set person. Climbing in a sewer probably wouldn't be her thing or mine."

"What about Dawn?"

Sandra opened her mouth.

Craig knew she was involved in the hoax.

"Look, I don't care what happened. I can't let them put you in prison."

"You think I'm guilty?"

Craig frowned. The meeting with Sandra wasn't going well.

"They will think you are guilty. The insurance company wants somebody to pay. They are going after you. I imagine Demonte Duran will have lots to tell them about your interest in Fiona once he finds out about your investments and the empty house. Let's not forget the missing jewelry."

Sandra realized she dragged Craig into her mess.

"Why do you care about what happens to me? You don't need to get involved. If the situation were reversed, I would run into the hills, kick the bear out, and hide in a cave for a year."

Craig watched her.

"You would leave me stranded?"

She refilled her cup with hot water and his with coffee. She moved the tea bags closer to her and nervously played with the packages.

"No, I would help you. I always help my close friends."

Craig walked over to his briefcase and pulled the black velvet box out. He walked back and got down on his knees.

"Marry me."

Sandra didn't move. There was no questioning tone to his words.

He opened the box.

"You are a very close friend."

Craig couldn't stand the suspense. Sandra wasn't reacting the way he wanted.

"How many nights did we make love?"

"Six."

He took the ring out of the slot and put the sparkly metal on her finger.

"I want more than six nights."

Sandra knew Craig was right about the investigation and police. He was also right about wanting more time with each other.

"Why?"

Craig showed her why he wanted her.

"Now, here's where we tell each other something special," said Craig

She nodded.

"I'll go first. I will love you forever and ever no matter how many secrets you have."

Sandra wiped her nose.

"I'll love you forever and ever and promise to be there."

"That's good enough for me."

Craig placed their suitcases in the rental car. He saw the white dress bag and box of wedding shoes. Danielle must have placed the gown in the vehicle. He might regret his quick decision. He saw Sandra turn to look at him. She hadn't gotten into the car. Sandra was pausing to reexamine the hasty marriage proposal.

"This is an emergency?"

He slammed the lid on the trunk.

"We are in a race before they issue me a subpoena."

She stopped him from opening her door.

"Look at this view. We'll have something crazy to tell our children about your wedding proposal."

Craig stopped and looked at the view. He was glad she mentioned children. There was no time like the present.

"We can work on those plans."

He tucked her in the front car seat and went to the driver's side. Craig drove them to the hotel.

Friday, Sandra Delray married Craig Connor in Rome with Danielle and her new boyfriend as witnesses. On Saturday, Craig flew back to Las Vegas.

As soon as the second rebuild house was completed, Sandra would return to the States. She promised him.

24 Fiona Moves

Danielle flew to Phoenix for a quick vacation. She talked with Dawn and Kim, Candy, and Darcy about the wedding and the impending possibility of more police activity on the Kendrell emerald heist. She laid out the game plan Sandra wanted them to follow.

Dawn, Kim, Candy, and Darcy were complete with their one and only rebuild house activity. Fiona graciously signed off from their investor loans. The women did own their properties free and clear.

Danielle and Sandra were pushing their contractors to get their last rebuild house completed.

Meanwhile, Fiona Kendrell stood in her living room in Los Angeles. She watched as the movers hauled away the few boxes of clothing and keepsakes. Her suitcase and Jarret's suitcase were waiting by the door for the airport limousine.

Fiona's house in Los Angeles was empty with newly painted walls. The clean carpet showed the huge effort required before the property could be rented. The maid cleaning service was there yesterday as was the gardener and pool people. The "For Rent" sign was on the front lawn.

"Well, Jarret, we succeeded in getting rid of this white elephant. I will be delighted to have a smaller home for a change. The first cottage in Rome looks charming. Our girls have moved into the next rebuild property."

"We did a lot of work. I'm happy to be moving to Rome."

"I did want to talk with you in case anything happens to me. My lawyer, Horatio approved. The cottage we will be living in is yours and an allowance to maintain and live there once I'm gone."

"Fiona, you don't have to take care of me. I have some money."

"I know but a little extra never hurts. Your loyalty surpasses the value of this property. Besides, I want you to be happy."

"Thank you."

The limousine arrived and took them to the airport. When they arrived in Rome, Danielle was waiting for them. A large rental car took them to their new home.

Fiona was ecstatic about the tiny house. Jarret liked his small space and balcony views. The women talked for hours about Sandra's marriage, Danielle's new boyfriend, a pool contractor, and the other problem.

"Demonte was furious with me. Unfortunately, he arrived as the cleaning people were done with the inside of my home. He threw a temper tantrum when he realized the furniture and artifacts were gone. He wanted to live in my house and not pay for anything. I told him now I can get money from my personal property and the rent to keep him in his little playboy world."

Danielle gritted her teeth.

"You didn't say, playboy?"

"I did. He's been a useless human being since his mother died. I did tell him he could have the house when I was gone. He demanded to see my will. I told him no."

"Good riddance," said Danielle.

The mover boxes would be delivered in a week.

Upon Sandra's return to Rome, the women planned outings. Fiona's weekly grocery delivery was set up. Jarret hired an additional meal service to deliver one meal a day for the two of them. She also hired a cleaning woman and driver service.

After two months, Craig flew back for a visit with his wife. He met Fiona again and went fishing with Jarret. Another month went by without incident.

25 Incident with Demonte

The second rebuild home was moving along nicely. The new floating lap pool was an engineering marvel. New landscaping dotted the backyard.

The pool cleaners left the circular driveway. A rental car pulled up to the house. The man assessed the property's value in a quick look around on the outside. He walked back around to the front door and walked into the home.

Sandra was eating her sandwich by the island in the kitchen. The man stopped and looked at his former girlfriend. She looked prettier and different.

Sandra turned and saw the man in a business suit. She would know him anywhere in a crowd.

"Demonte, I heard you might pay your aunt a visit. How nice to see you?"

He walked around the interior of the house examining the wood, fireplaces, and construction.

"Since when do you know about rebuilding houses? I saw the dump you put my aunt and her butler in. Why isn't she in this home?"

Sandra knew their seeing each other again would be a bad thing. His negative attitude would always be present.

"This house is not yet livable."

"How long before this house is done?"

Sandra wasn't sure why he was interested in her plans.

"We think three to five months. It all depends on the inspection process."

She followed him around the inside of the home. He wiped the dust off the fireplace in the master bedroom. His hands were dirty.

"You should have called me," said Demonte.

Sandra racked her brain about why she should have contacted him.

"I beg your pardon."

"The emeralds and diamonds, Sandra. You do remember my aunt's collection. As I recall, you did a little research about the gems after her show. Do you know which show I'm talking about? Now I know why you were intrigued and put your hooks into me."

Sandra opened her mouth to reply with a retort and stopped herself.

"I'm sorry about your aunt's jewelry. I know she loved wearing the pieces her husband gave her."

"You didn't say the jewelry was gone. Did she or you hide them somewhere?"

Sandra was done with being polite.

"Get the heck off my property."

Demonte exploded.

"Your property? My mother told me she invested four million dollars in this beast. Next, she mentioned how she helped your club friends. How did you manage to convince her of the benefits of such crooked schemes? Obviously, you have found a demon lawyer to help."

She didn't want to tell him her firm used Horatio Golden.

"You've worked Fiona and her generosity to a pulp. I should never have brought you to her home. You took advantage of me and now her. I don't see how you can stand yourself."

Sandra's eyes burned.

"Don't you dare talk to me about using someone. Every time I visit, she's given you another two or three million. We have a contract and will pay her back for the loan. You never pay her back."

Demonte moved to the doorway blocking her exit.

"She's my next of kin. You are nobody."

"Get out of my way."

Suddenly he grabbed Sandra by the throat and slammed her against the open door. Her hands grasped for the knob to steady herself.

"You don't get to tell me to move. Again, let me reiterate my previous thoughts. You are nobody. I've gone to a lawyer to stop this terrible charade of yours. My aunt is senile and her current contract with you will be canceled. I repeat, canceled. I've also talked to an insurance man by the name of Reginald North about the jewelry. He was very interested in what I had to say."

They both heard a revolver click.

"Step away from her, Demonte, or I'll blow more than your head off."

"Danielle, I didn't hear you come in. Oh, my god, you do have a revolver. Are you crazy? Guns must be illegal here."

Danielle smiled wickedly,

"What do you care? You'll be dead. Let me repeat myself. You'll be very dead. Nobody will care."

Demonte moved away from the door and let Sandra pass. Danielle motioned for him to move to the front door.

Upon reaching the open door, he stopped.

"I'm going to sue you both."

Danielle moved quickly to block his exit. The tables were now turned on him.

"I believe you need to retract that last statement. I know where you live."

Demonte looked drily at Sandra.

Danielle didn't budge and stood her ground. They heard Danielle's muscular boyfriend ride into the drive and park his motorbike. He came to the door and saw the scene.

"Danielle put away the gun. Man, that's the third time this week some asshole has pissed her off."

Demonte's face dropped. He hastily retreated to his rental car when Danielle turned toward her boyfriend.

"Hi, Hank, look what you've done. You've spoiled my day."

Danielle's boyfriend grinned.

"Anybody want donuts?"

Danielle looked at Sandra, "You need to call Craig and tell him about this asshole."

Sandra turned and went back into the kitchen. She grabbed her cell phone, walked into the bathroom, and threw up.

When she hit the send button, Craig immediately picked up her call.

"Craig, we had a tiny incident today with Demonte. His unhappiness hit an all-time high. I'm fine."

Craig tapped his ink pen on his wooden desk.

"Is he still there?"

"No, he has left. We should have installed the front door lock. I'll get someone over tomorrow."

"I'll have someone from the hotel come over today. You do have the lock device at the house?"

"Yes, it's inside the front door."

"Okay, sweetheart. I will call you this evening."

Craig walked into the security room of the Las Vegas hotel with the cameras.

Kevin saw the look on the boss's face.

"Somebody is pissed."

"Sandra's ex-boyfriend showed up at the building site today."

"And everything is fine?" said Kevin.

"I don't know. She sounded quiet or something."

"If it was my wife, I would contact her best friend in the world to find out the true facts and events that occurred."

"Thank you, Kevin."

"My pleasure."

26 Fiona Trouble

The next day Demonte drove his rental car to the small house by the ocean to talk with Fiona. He was surprised to see Jarret was not there.

"Demonte, why don't you entertain yourself and see some of the sights in Rome. You could visit a cathedral and pray for your soul."

"Very funny, Fiona. Your virtues aren't exactly glowing. My mother told me about some of the stunts you played. One of them was called *the disappearing act*."

"Yes, I miss your mother. We made a neighbor's pet rabbit disappear for a week."

"I came by today to let you know I'll be back in a month or two after I get my poor wife settled into a different place."

Fiona motioned for him to get her a water bottle from the refrigerator. He handed her the bottle.

"I didn't know you were moving."

"We're moving into your rental in LA. I had my lawyer write up a letter to kick the current couple out of the house due to their negligence. They were happy to leave."

Fiona felt sad for her renters. They didn't deserve to be harassed. They weren't in the house but a month.

She mustered her courage.

"If you move into my house without my authorization, I will ask my lawyer to call the police. You will be accused of trespassing."

"You can't kick me out."

Fiona looked outside. She only wanted peace.

"All right, we make a deal. I'll have my lawyer gift you the house."

Demonte knew the gift tax laws. He would have to pay taxes.

"The house is in my name on your estate?"

"The LA house is in only your name on my estate."

Demonte looked at the long steps to the beach.

"We should leave the situation regarding the LA house alone."

Fiona hadn't been feeling well lately.

"I will not change anything."

"The house rebuild contract with Danielle and Sandra must be canceled."

Fiona looked at Demonte.

"No, I won't cancel the contract. Stop pushing, Demonte."

Demonte still didn't know where the money from the emeralds stood.

"What about the money from the insurance?"

"I'm tired today. We'll talk more next time." She patted his hand.

Jarret opened the door and deposited the small bag of groceries for the week on the counter. He didn't like Fiona's nephew and the feelings were mutual. He stood staring with his hands on his hips.

"Put the milk away, Jarret." Demonte stomped out the door.

Fiona let out her breath.

"Don't worry; he will return in a month or two. Let's hope the date is the latter one."

Jarret opened the ice cream and put two scoops in a bowl and poured strawberry topping on the inside of the dish. He carried the bowl to Fiona.

"Thank you."

"Did he want more money?"

Fiona knew her butler was wanting an answer.

"Today Demonte asked about the insurance money. He also reminded me of a game his mother and I played."

Jarret sat down on the couch.

"The white rabbit story is hilarious." Fiona licked her spoon.

"I don't think the police would be amused that we lost the rabbit and took our allowance to buy a new one. We couldn't believe the rabbit disappeared. Later we found the lost rabbit five miles away at Henderson's house. We had to switch them. It was the right thing to do."

"Unfortunately, I can't switch the emeralds and diamonds."

Jarret knew some parts of the law.

"What if they are found after your death? Sandra could convince the women."

Fiona thought about Jarret's comment.

"Wouldn't everyone have a field day with your idea?"

"You could have pulled the heist by yourself or Jim possibly helped you. We do have a picture of the tea cart from the auction house."

"What about the ladders and gloves?"

Jarret took the empty bowls and washed them in the sink.

"Easy. Workers leave tools and gloves behind all the time."

"Brilliant! I feel better already."

27 North's Speculation

A piece of paper was put in Mr. North's in-basket at work. He reached for the item and read the information.

He rolled back his chair.

"I'll be damned. This complicates my investigation."

He looked at the number of times Sandra Delray stayed at the two hotels. She was there a total of two times and one overnight across the street.

"Mr. Connor. You move fast. My suspect doesn't need to worry about your testimony."

He shuffled his new notes into six piles. The insurance investigator still didn't have solid evidence.

"Each woman currently works in order to survive. They obviously all met through some grief support group. The word grief alone would give a jury the sympathetic vote. Average working women were a few more words he could throw in their favor. They took their life savings and came to Las Vegas for fun and the glamorous shows. Vegas casinos love these groups."

Moving a few pages aside, he scanned over the financial figures. He looked at their investments.

"Fiona loaned them money which four of them paid back. Ms. Kendrell is known for her high donations to the church and people in need. Ding, ding, more bonus points for the six women and our victim."

He pulled out the interview with the ex-boyfriend of Sandra Delray.

"The man hates the woman. Every sentence Mr. Duran speaks is trash-talking and crap. He sponges off Ms. Kendrell and is a rat. Every sentence Ms. Delray utters will be nice and sweet on the stand in the courtroom. Then there's the smart and pretty look. All I need now is for her to be pregnant. Ding, dang, dong. Ms. Delray wins the next round."

He lifted the marriage license.

"The man, Craig Connor, is a manager and runs a profitable hotel. All the businessmen in town think he's tops. He loves his new bride and won't testify against her. Boom, the confetti drops. The jury cheers. The newlyweds win the game."

"Arrggghh?"

People in the insurance office stopped working. This was the second time this week, Mr. North was going ape shit.

People started whispering behind his back and giving each other worried looks.

"The jewels are the key. Who made the perfect fakes?"

Reginald looked at the pictures the Las Vegas photographer took.

"Nothing wrong with any of these pictures. Mr. Sloan went to display fourteen. We have a picture of fourteen."

He threw his heavy metal holder of pencils at his door. There was an exceptionally loud thud. The school-bus colored pencils rolled out under his door into the hallway.

Looking at the jewel case on his desk with rocks that equaled the weight of the jewels, he agreed. Ms. Kendrell would have a hard time lifting the case. Jim Sloan wouldn't have. Reginald pushed the case with his foot. The case moved easily.

He went over to his small refrigerator and took out a cola. Unscrewing the cap, he took a swallow. Reginald pushed the case with his hands. The case slid easily.

"Maybe someone switched the carts."

He opened his door and picked up the pencils. He closed the door and took one pencil at a time and threw the pointed pencils. The pencils hit the outside of the box and bounced to the floor.

"If Jim switched the box, our company loses. If Fiona or Sandra switched the box, we win. Sandra wasn't at the house. The judge dismisses the case."

He groaned.

"Speculation is not evidence."

Reginald selected more cola bottles out of the cold box and sat them on his desk.

"Table, jewels, tea cart. Fiona, and Jim."

His manager opened the door with what looked like a bomb squad person.

"Go home, Reginald. You can clean up this mess in the morning. Come to my office for a meeting tomorrow at nine regarding the search warrant on Ms. Kendrell's lockboxes. Don't throw that heavy pencil holder at the glass door. My secretary thought a bomb went off when everyone scrambled under their desks. The tenants in the next building heard the hit and saw the confusion through the windows. They called the bomb people."

Reginald put the offensive pencil holder in a desk drawer.

"Yes, sir."

His manager stopped.

"Reginald?"

Reginald looked at his boss.

"No more groaning."

His manager shut the door. Reginald lost his concentration. He felt a glimmer of light at the end of a tunnel before he was interrupted. The light or flicker of an idea was gone.

He opened his desk drawer. The car keys were missing. Reginald always put his keys in the drawer. He panicked until the ring clinked by his foot. Reginald found them on the floor with yellow pencils.

"There are spirits in this room. They moved my keys."

28 Vegas Lawyer Letter

Demonte came home to see his wife standing in the driveway holding a letter and envelope by the mailbox. He parked the car in his garage and waited for his wife.

She blew past him into the house. When he walked in the kitchen, his wife was standing with her arms crossed and an ugly look appeared on her face.

"Read the letter, stupid."

The stationery looked like lawyer paper. He wondered what Fiona was up to now.

The lawyers' names on the envelope were from Las Vegas.

"Did you get in an accident in Vegas?"

She shook her head and pointed at the letter.

"All right. I'm reading this strange lawyer letter."

He put the paper down.

"We had a misunderstanding."

His wife was in his face.

"You went to see Sandra behind my back. You told me she was nobody. Yet, you met with her in Rome, unknown to your wife. I want to hear your explanation. I'm sure the meeting was by accident."

"She's trying to rebuild a house. Fiona gave her some of our money. Fiona said it was a loan. Four million dollars out of our inheritance is not good. I told Fiona to withdraw the loan. But first, I went to see the rebuilt house. Sandra was there. I can't have Fiona wasting our money on Sandra's projects. I also needed to ask Fiona and Sandra about the emeralds. They never told us about the theft. There is something sneaky going on with the two of them. We shouldn't have stayed away. Sandra has developed a neat foothold into our nest egg."

"I am sick and tired of hearing about those stupid stones and your ex-girlfriend. So, what if Fiona did a loan! People must pay back a loan even if they are dead. What about the bronze statues I wanted?"

"They are gone."

"I told you we should have taken the statues the last time we visited. No, you wanted to wait. I listened to you. Now, we have Sandra's husband, and I repeat, rich husband, wanting to sue us because you hit his wife!"

"I didn't hit her. I choked her."

"That is pathetic."

"Look, she made me mad."

"Big deal. You make me mad. I
don't choke you even though I want to right
here in this ugly kitchen. I hate this kitchen."

"This letter doesn't talk about the
scare I ran into at the rebuilt house in Rome.
Danielle pulled a revolver on me."

"Good for her. Too bad she didn't
use the gun."

"Fiona wasn't even very nice to me.
You're not nice to me."

His wife threw the frozen lump of
hamburger in the kitchen sink.

"I have to cook cheap tacos and
canned beans in this depressing house in old
clothes. Every day, I watch your children.
She eats in fancy restaurants. They both eat
better food than I do. You better get your act
together and don't let Fiona off the hook.
Fiona hates me and always wins because
you don't stand up to her."

Demonte didn't have any money for
lawyers or bronzes without Fiona's
generosity.

"Fiona likes you. She's going to put
the LA house in her estate in my name."

Demonte's wife caught the
inference.

"My name is not going to be on the
house papers?"

Demonte bit his fingernail.

"I'll go to my lawyer and see what I can do."

His wife pushed her finger into the hamburger, ripping the plastic wrap.

"I want him to call the auction place, too. We might find the statues."

"Okay, but we'll have to pay two hundred fifty dollars an hour for the call."

"You pay the money. My check from work goes into my account."

29 Second Renovation

Sandra and Danielle helped Fiona in the wheelchair. There was a temporary wood ramp to the house for the chair wheels.

"Open your eyes, Fiona. Here is the front of the home."

She clapped her hands.

"The wrought iron looks arabesque. The yellow color is beautiful."

They wheeled her inside. The floors were marble. The kitchen and family room were one large space overlooking the hills. In the distance, you could see the water.

"This area is casual and fun."

They wheeled her to the large master bedroom, bath, and closet area. She approved the white satin bedspread and black velvet headboard with matching chairs. The other master bedroom wasn't as large as the other one and there was a small library.

The piece de la resistance was the lap pool. The pool was shallow enough for a person to stand.

"This is where I would like to be during the day if I lived here. The pool is lovely."

They went back to the family room.

"I like the size, not too big or too small."

They escorted her into the kitchen where Jarret was waiting.

"You women have done a really great job with this house."

"Thanks, Jarret," said Sandra.

They sat down to hot tea and bakery scones with butter.

Fiona was having a good time.

"I'm glad I could help your group of women to achieve a better life. You all have worked hard to accomplish your desires and conquer your fears. I'm very proud. My last years have been memorable. The emeralds were the stars in my life. The money will help many people."

Both Danielle and Sandra gave Fiona a hug and hugs for Jarret.

"I'll contact Horatio to draw up the paperwork. Once the home is sold, he can quickly close our loan contract."

"Are you sure you don't want to move into this home?"

"Danielle, I'm content with my cottage by the ocean. There aren't as many steps to walk. Jarret is all right with the house. He's gotten familiar with the neighbors and the shop owners. I'm not far from my friends and good food. There is nothing more that I require."

Sandra looked at Danielle. When this house sold, Sandra would return to live with Craig.

"Both of you women need the money from the sale so you can go your separate ways. Danielle wants a small tourist shop in this city and Sandra needs to be closer to Craig. Now, can I go home?"

"Of course, the car is out front. Danielle can lock the house and turn on the security alarm with her phone."

Sandra waited alone with Fiona. She talked about her funeral and ashes. Sandra was alarmed about Fiona's health.

"Don't worry. My ending has already been written. Horatio has all the details. I do want to tell you about the emeralds. Jarret has a brilliant plan."

"Why don't I stop by tomorrow for lunch? I'll bring us corned beef sandwiches with swiss cheese from the deli. Yes, I'll remember the pickles."

"I'll be waiting for you," said Fiona.

Sandra watched as Danielle drove away with her occupants toward the city. She climbed into her car and drove to the small apartment she and Danielle rented until the house was sold. The realtor sign would be placed on the property in the morning.

Sandra called Craig when she arrived home.

"Sweetheart, how was Fiona's tour?"

"She was happy but will stay in the little cottage. I'll see her tomorrow for lunch. She wants to talk to me privately."

"Should I be concerned?"

Sandra thought about Fiona.

"I'm fine. I think Fiona might not be feeling well."

"I'm sorry to hear her health is a bother. Give her my best."

"I will."

"Goodnight love."

Sandra could hardly wait to be in Vegas.

"Love you, too."

30 Lunch with Fiona

The drive was short to Fiona's cottage. Jarret opened the door. He was leaving to go for a walk.

"Sandra, come in."

Fiona quipped, "I'm hungry."

She placed the sandwiches on paper plates and brought the orange juice to the table.

"Have you been feeling well, dear?"

Sandra's forehead wrinkled.

"Don't frown so much dear. Wrinkles are a terrible thing and only look good on dogs. The dermatologists have dog pictures in their places of business to encourage women to buy more product."

Sandra laughed. She saw a few dog breeds that fit the bill.

"I was going to ask you the same question. You seemed out of sorts toward the end of last evening."

"I know. We'll talk about the emeralds later. They are what is weighing on your mind. First, we talk about you."

"I'm getting dizzy in the morning. I'll go into my doctor in about two weeks for my normal checkup."

"Tell him you are going to have a daughter."

Sandra's eyes blinked.

"What daughter?"

Fiona sat back and swallowed her bite of corned beef.

"I can tell that you are pregnant."

Sandra was mentally checking her calendar.

"Now that you mention it, I am two weeks late."

"See, women know these things. Congratulations! You'll be wanting more weird food other than dill pickles."

"Oh, Fiona, this will be another scary project."

"You will do everything perfectly, most of the time. Just don't buy her a rabbit. They multiply."

"Now, what are you going to do about the emeralds?" asked Sandra.

They discussed the pros and cons for over an hour.

"You ran the important questions past your lawyer. The questions were hypothetical. The trouble that might occur down the road if anyone knew would be bad."

"Yes. Horatio is a dear friend and is working items I mentioned as we speak. He doesn't really know what happened with regards to the emeralds. He's also flying here to work on my funeral requests and my estate."

"I'm absolutely overwhelmed by the amount of work you have completed," said Sandra.

Fiona finished the last bite of her sandwich.

"Thank you, dear."

She handed Sandra her scrapbook. Sandra slowly turned the pages of yellowed newspaper clippings. This was Fiona's life. Her hands stopped. Sandra looked at Fiona in shock.

"You must keep our meeting information today to yourself. Keep things brief with Craig. However, I do have a favor."

Sandra sighed, "My violin playing?"

"Yes. Your lessons begin tomorrow. I understand he is a top-notch teacher. I only hire the best. The orchestra has been booked for some pre-rehearsals and then booked for my future funeral. Tents are in the order in case of rain. I promised them that I wouldn't die on a weekend. If I did, there are refrigerators."

Sandra started to cry.

"I shouldn't have mentioned the cooling items. I forget the young are sensitive. Don't waste your tears on me. Old people do die. It's good to preplan. I love you like a daughter, too, Sandra. The future is in your hands. I know you can complete the mission. The heist was a perfect example of your intelligence."

The two women wiped their tears before Jarret could see them upon his return. The future was rolling rapidly toward Fiona's final days.

Sandra couldn't tell Craig. He noticed on their last visit that she was gaining weight.

She told him, "Too many brioche rolls from the bakery."

Sandra was surprised he believed her.

31 Horatio Visits Fiona

The photographer left Fiona's
cottage and drove away. Another car pulled
into her driveway and an elderly man
stepped out. Jarret shook hands with Horatio
and showed him the doorway. Jarret went
for his daily walk.

Fiona's face brightened when she
saw her lawyer. He took her cool hands in
his warm ones. He noticed she was wearing
a nice evening two-piece outfit during the
day.

"My photographer was here to take
some portraits."

"You look great for someone who is
suddenly ill."

"Shh, be quiet. My being ill is a
secret, except for Jarret. Thank you for
coming. Your wife stayed in London?"

"Yes, she will fly to New York to
stay with her son for a week. I'll be flying to
LA to deal with your lockboxes."

Fiona nodded. "I knew the police
and Mr. North would eventually turn their
eyes in my direction. Jim and I supposedly
were the last ones to see my emeralds. The
first bank box contains old insurance papers,
birth and marriage certificates. A copy of

my old will is in the box and should be destroyed. The other bank box is one I established before the jewelry show. I brought a bronze statue of mine to Las Vegas. The statue is two small deer about six inches high by nine inches long. I brought the bronze to the show to sell. The dealer bowed out of the sale. I asked Sandra to return the bronze to the bank deposit box when she left Vegas. She told me that I should let my nephew's wife have the object when I have passed away. She said the statue would appease Petrissa and would be a goodwill gesture. I've thought about the deer and I would like her to have the bronze as a gift before I die."

"It's good to know what is in your lockboxes before the police make me be present for their opening. There's no way we can get out of their search warrant on the bank boxes. I'll have the bronze wrapped and shipped to Petrissa. Do you know the value for insurance purposes?"

Fiona thought about the estimate she received five years ago.

"The range was fifty to sixty thousand dollars. The artist is well-known and only made a few of the bronzes. A high dollar might be seventy-five thousand."

The lawyer wrote notes in his black book.

185

"What else do we need to take care of today? Your funeral plans are all arranged. Your ashes will be in a white marble rabbit urn. The urn will be given to Jarret. I understand Sandra will be your administrator. I have made the change and have the papers here for your signature."

"You didn't ask me about the rabbit urn. There's a story about white rabbits. I thought Jarret would get a kick out of the urn. I wanted to make him smile. You have my request to donate the rest of my money from the insurance claim to the charities immediately. We have calculated the rest of my expenses, the funeral costs, and medical bills to allow me to live comfortably."

"Yes, we will keep a safe million in your savings for any emergency."

Fiona looked at the ocean.

"Sandra and Danielle are taking me to the beach next week so I can get my feet wet. I expect the day will be fun."

Horatio went to the refrigerator and helped himself to the lemonade. He held the jug up. Fiona shook her head. She preferred her water. Horatio sat down.

"This cottage suits you. However, there is one last gift that should be completed."

"Yes. I have briefly mentioned we stored some items and were planning on moving them here once I was settled."

Fiona handed her lawyer the manifest from the shipper of the items in storage in Los Angeles. He read off the items.

"There is an antique tea cart, full silver tea service, twenty-four-service of good china with serving pieces, and crystal."

Fiona smiled.

"We used to have large parties and used the good china."

Horatio continued reading.

"The list shows a Federal Style bedroom set which is a highboy, bedposts and rails, a large low chest, a mirror for the low chest, and a bedside chest. Next, we have boxes of wedding and baby photos, some more bronzes, lamps, and two paintings. The green dress is interesting."

"Yes. Now everything in this storage space is my additional wedding gift to Sandra. She currently only knows about the tea service and cart."

Horatio took the list and put it in his briefcase. He wrote on the document prepared for Sandra's gift to add the storage items as an addendum. He had Fiona initial and sign all his documents.

"I believe we are done with your wishes. I will let you know when all the gifts have been acknowledged."

Fiona took her dear friend's hand.

"We will miss you."

"I do know. There is something else that's been bothering me."

Horatio went to the refrigerator and refilled his glass. He took a few cookies out of the bag in the refrigerator and handed two to his good friend.

"For five years now, I have been forgetting things. The doctors told me the forgetfulness was the start of my tumor growing. There would be days that went by and I couldn't remember them. I would ask Jarret to fill in the gaps."

"I'm sorry to hear you were struggling for that long."

Fiona ate her cookie.

"I think I made an error in telling Mr. North about a possible copy of my emeralds. My husband was a very cautious man at times. Some people would say he was shrewd. He might have made a copy of the collection. There is one necklace which he gave me right before he died."

Fiona handed a yellowed newspaper clipping of her at a garden party function.

Mr. Golden looked at the necklace.

"I remember this annual rose function. My wife commented on the large emerald cut diamond center of the necklace. There were good quality emeralds surrounding the stone in the white gold setting. The chain was superb and the matching earrings incredible. This necklace was not part of the emerald collection. Do you still own the necklace?"

Fiona frowned.

"There is the reason why I called you. The dilemma bothers me. I believe the necklace is in storage with my things. I put a note on the outside of the velvet. The necklace is a gift for Sandra for her help. The New York Jeweler's name is still on this one bag. I keep seeing the original bags aligned in two rows. If we find the diamond necklace, we can check with the jeweler company to see if their records still exist."

Horatio found the document for Sandra and added addendum B on the document and the newspaper clipping. Fiona initialed both.

"I think we are done," said Fiona.

"Mr. North seemed a little frazzled when I talked with him on the phone. I believe the investigation and lack of finding your emeralds have taken over his life. Do you think the emeralds will ever be found?"

Fiona smiled. "They are like the white rabbit."

"You believe the green emeralds will show themselves."

She watched as Horatio put the papers in his briefcase.

"I do."

He snapped the locks shut and watched his client. Horatio knew Fiona for years. He wasn't about to question her judgment now.

"Your halo is still there when I look at you. I'll put ten million as the value on Sandra's wedding gifts. I know the paintings are worth a good seven hundred fifty thousand and the necklace is probably close to five. I could raise the figure?"

"No, the amount is close enough."

"Is there any change in the amount to your nephew? He will be upset that you have gifted away most everything except the house in Los Angeles. I know you haven't told him about your illness."

"You have the list of checks I have given Demonte over the years. The amount is substantial. Plus, my husband bought their current home for them before he died. Then there's the buffer of a million dollars in the estate. It's time for Demonte to make his own way. He doesn't know I'm ill."

"All right. I wanted to be sure."

"Bless you, Horatio. Tell Gretchen thanks for letting you visit with me. I hope I didn't interrupt your vacation too much."

"Don't you worry about us. Good day. You take care and have fun at the beach."

Horatio left the cottage as Jarret returned. They chatted for ten minutes before the lawyer left.

32 Mr. North's Job

Reginald watched as did Horatio as the lady brought the heavy lockbox to the table. She opened the box.

Horatio smiled as she lifted the fragile bronze out of the box. The soft layer of blue velvet was underneath the statue. Reginald looked in the empty box and then he turned the bronze over. There were no jewels in the box or underneath the small object. He felt the velvet. The box was a bust.

"Cute deer. The design of the two babies licking each other is soothing. What do you think Mr. North?"

The bank lady saw all kinds of things in bank boxes. This object beat all the others in the thrilling, *what's in the box game*?

"The bronze can go back," said Mr. North.

Horatio opened his briefcase and handed the signed document to the police officer who gave the document to the bank lady.

"I'll get the paperwork to close out the lockbox and her account."

Horatio pulled the flat mailing box and bubble wrap out along with the heavy tape. He started putting the box together. The police officer helped him put the object inside with the bubble wrap. Horatio taped the box shut.

"I might need some help in getting the box to my car. Is there a cart around?"

The bank lady handed him the papers and went to get a cart.

"Ms. Kendrell gave you the statue."

"Oh, no, the statue is a gift for her nephew's wife. I'm to either mail or drop the box off at the house. We can go check the other bank box. I'll meet you inside the bank."

The second box contained old paperwork and no emeralds.

Reginald watched as the bank lady went to get the closing paperwork. Horatio stuffed the papers in an envelope and placed the envelope in his briefcase.

"Good day, Mr. North."

Reginald walked with the policeman to his vehicle.

"We are done with the search warrant on the lockboxes. I'll turn in my report, Mr. North."

Reginald sat in his car. He was afraid to return to work. Slowly, he drove from Los Angeles to his home. In the morning, he went into his insurance company's office as usual and stepped inside his room. He left the door open. The piles of paper were missing from his desk.

The papers were like his keys. He must have put the papers away or the evil spirits were in his office again. Reginald turned to look at the other workers. No one would look at him.

His manager's secretary stood in the doorway next to the agent. She informed Reginald there was a meeting in the boss's office.

"Take your briefcase with you."

Reginald wondered why he needed his briefcase.

His manager was sitting with the personnel woman. Reginald gulped and loosened his tie.

After thirty minutes, he was escorted out of the insurance building. His company told him the needs of the business had changed. His one large insurance case was now officially closed with the insurance company and filed as a lost cause. The other agents took up the slack. His job was over. They let Reginald retire.

He drove home and sat in his driveway until the neighborhood kid's basketball hit his car.

"That does it."

Reginald got out of the car and put the basketball in the trunk. Then he drove out into a deserted area. He opened the trunk and threw the basketball as far as he could.

"I'll probably have to pay for a new ball. No, let the mother buy the brat another ball. A fence. I could build a fence on my property. No, the ball will come over the fence. Think, Reginald, how do you lose a ball? Simple. You turn the ball into jewels. Jewels always disappear. No, people make jewels disappear just like you did with the basketball."

Slowly, Reginald's brain started churning away again. He got back into his car and drove home. He popped popcorn, watched detective movies, and grew a beard. Then Reginald got a bright idea. He went to his safe.

33 Doctor's Visit

By the time Sandra saw her doctor, she calculated maybe she was a month pregnant. Sandra was shocked when he told her that she was not. He told her the body sometimes gave out false signals and didn't always cooperate. Plus, she appeared to be dehydrated. He recommended she drink more water.

She called Fiona to tell her the news.

"I specifically dreamed of a wonderful story about you being pregnant. The dream was clear as a bell. You wore a black dress and looked very pretty. Your necklace was white pearls with an emerald and there were matching earrings. Music was in the air. I could hear people talking and they appeared to be enjoying themselves."

"How very odd? I usually have dreams, too. Then I wake up and the magic is gone."

Fiona knew Sandra was disappointed about no future happenings with the baby route.

"I have an excellent idea. Why don't you take a couple of weeks off or at least a month? Fly to Las Vegas and take a short honeymoon with your handsome husband."

Sandra liked the idea.

"What about my violin lessons?"

"You can do them online. The instructor has several students who go to a rental studio and play their lessons. He listens to their music and gives them feedback."

Sandra suddenly knew there was a reason she should visit Craig.

"I need to relax. Danielle can handle the real estate person while I'm away."

"Go, be gone with you. Jarret and I are capable of handling things. Danielle is here if we need her."

Sandra hung up the call and rang another number.

Craig was delighted and would pick her up at the Las Vegas airport. He would take some days off when she hinted her stay might be a month. He told her a month would be appreciated immensely.

She didn't tell him about the false alarm nor Fiona's strange dream.

Danielle was ready to drive her to the airport in Rome.

"Are you okay? Your face for a minute was sad."

"I'm a little off. Fiona noticed and pushed me to take better care of myself. Her remedy was to spend more time with Craig. I was thinking of taking two weeks. She recommended a month."

"I don't know, a month's worth of sleepless nights could have the opposite effect."

Sandra picked up her purse and checked her tickets.

"We sleep."

Danielle gave her a look.

"Right, ten minutes after breakfast."

34 Craig and Sandra

He kissed her before she could talk. "I'm so glad you decided to take time off. This being apart was driving me insane. I need a warm body close to me."

Sandra knew what he meant. She also was unhappy about their living arrangements.

"I saw the video of your completed rebuild. Good contractor work on the pool design. The pool alone should sell the property."

"We do have a couple interested. They want a larger house and are looking at ways the house might be expanded."

"Great, let's get you home. First, we stop at the hotel so you can meet my security guard, Kevin Meadow. I talk about you all the time and he wanted to see you in person instead of on our cameras."

"I would love to meet Kevin."

He drove in the underground parking and they walked through the doors to the elevator. He took his badge and flashed the door. The light appeared and he opened the door to a room with a massive display of screens.

"Wow, this room looks complicated."

A man came over to the two of them. Craig made introductions.

"I finally get to meet Sandra Delray and the now Mrs. Connor. I would recognize you anywhere."

Sandra knew her red suit made an immediate impact.

"I'm pleased to see you in your work environment. Craig tells me your wife likes to shop. I would like to take her shopping and do lunch while I'm here."

Kevin was ecstatic.

"I will have her call you. She wants to visit Europe someday. Craig gave me your cell phone number."

"Okay, enough talking, I'm taking the rest of the day off to spend time with my beautiful wife."

Craig ushered Sandra out of the room.

"I wanted to see the equipment and systems first."

"No, I don't think so. The more you know about hotel systems, the more you can get into trouble."

"Hmmm, you are no fun."

Craig adored Sandra but sometimes he needed to be careful. He shouldn't have allowed her past the security door.

"We'll see how you answer the fun question tomorrow."

She grabbed his arm and snuggled close.

"I like when you try to scare me."

Her spirits were lifted after seeing her husband. He looked excited, too. She wondered what lied ahead for them. She hoped Mr. North never found the truth regarding the missing emeralds. Someday Craig might see the originals. Now was not a good time to tell him. Never was a better concept.

"Mr. North pushed for a warrant to see Fiona's bank lockboxes."

Craig unlocked the penthouse. They stepped inside.

"Really. They are also looking at Fiona?"

"Yes. She told me what was in her lockboxes. I already knew what was in one of them."

Craig's brow wrinkled.

"A small bronze and the other box contain old papers."

"I'm sure the lack of jewels will not go over very big with the insurance company."

"You are correct on that score. She asked me to be her administrator when she passes on."

Craig put his coat in the closet and took her suitcase into the bedroom so she could unpack. He sat down on the bed and watched her put things in drawers.

"She gave me pictures of the tea cart and the silver service she has given us for our wedding. Here is the auctioneer's estimate."

Craig looked at the pictures and the estimate. His head jerked and he looked at his wife.

"Yes, the cart alone is worth a million dollars."

He looked again at the cart. "This is like the one we saw at a shop in Rome. Only this model is different. The lower space is larger so the height must be higher."

"Did you find a recording space for me?"

Craig disappeared and returned with the card.

"Here's the address. She changed her estate papers and put you in as the executor over Demonte?"

"Her words were, you are smarter, my dear."

Craig smiled.

"I agree with her wholeheartedly. You're also very sexy in red."

He approached. She was halfway unpacked.

"We could throw the suitcase on the floor," said Craig.

"Or I could unpack, and we could eat dinner."

He called the restaurant.

"We have a table. Let's get the food business out of the way."

He took her hand and they walked together. The hotel was filling up with tourists this time of day. They needed to eat early because the restaurant would have lines forming fast.

Later in the evening, she told him about her false alarm. Craig held her tight.

"I'm all right with however long we take to have a family. We've been busy and rushing across two continents. Stress is more than likely a factor. We go slow in the baby-making business."

Sandra was glad she shared at least this piece. She didn't tell him Fiona told her where the proximity of the emeralds might be. Fiona would leave her two clues.

Craig watched his wife. Something more than a baby was causing her thoughts to drift.

"Is there anything else?"

She needed to tell him, but she stopped. It was not her place to divulge the information. The less Craig knew, the better. There was one other problem.

"I think Fiona is very ill."

Craig was not surprised.

"I'm sure her doctors are doing what's necessary."

Sandra became distressed.

"You aren't listening."

Craig stopped caressing his wife.

"Did she say she was ill?"

"No, she wouldn't. Fiona is very good about keeping secrets."

Craig knew someone else who also kept secrets.

"Is there anything we can do?"

Sandra sighed.

"She told me she was happy, but I know something is wrong. I think she was trying to prepare me for her exit."

"Hey, being upset is normal. Fiona obviously loves you very much and wants you to be happy. Did you know she ran a background check on me before we knew each other?"

It was Sandra's turn to be surprised.

"Seriously?"

"She told me that I would be a good candidate for you if I was looking for a wife. Fiona showed me your picture when she stayed once at our hotel. When I saw you in the Green Room for the first time, I knew who you were."

"Is that why you were suspicious of me."

"No, you walked differently."

"Is there some security manual that targets a model's walk?"

Craig didn't want to go into details of his original thoughts about her. He needed to get her off the conversation about the model-look or this evening would be destroyed.

"I didn't like the other guy hitting on you when you were in my hotel."

Sandra smiled remembering. She understood male turf-war. All the hotel's hidden cameras were also revealed. That must have hurt his ego. She also knew her husband wouldn't reveal any more security ideas to her.

"I'm glad she checked on your background. You are right, Fiona wants to make me happy."

"Can we stop talking and work on relaxing? I want to find that happy place, too."

Sandra relaxed in her husband's arms. Fiona was a romantic and loved the feeling of true love. Sandra was warming to the concept. They were young with years of

living ahead of them. She wasn't going to
waste the time by worrying anymore.

"Talking is all done until after coffee
for breakfast."

35 Auction House Call

Reginald North was retired but he could still investigate the missing jewels on his own time. He called the realtor regarding Fiona's property rental in Los Angeles.

"I'm sorry, Ms. Kendrell's house is rented for the next three years. We were lucky to find a client long term."

"Darn, my friend really liked the location. I'll tell them to keep looking. They do have a realtor already."

The realtor didn't have any other listings in the area.

"You know. My friend also is looking to buy quality furniture. They like the older styles. I know sometimes people use auction houses to sell their furniture when they leave town. Maybe your client used an auction house on her stuff. If you have the name, my friend would be forever thankful."

"I can give you three different auction houses that are very good with clients in this price category."

"Great, let me give you my personal email address."

Reginald called all three auction places. They never heard of Ms. Kendrell. He was stumped. One of the auction houses gave him a website of high quality and reputable dealers. He looked at the items on the website and didn't find what he was looking for. He dialed the number.

"I'm looking for a tea cart for my friend. They can afford the best and have very expensive tastes."

George from the auction website responded, "You will want the wood ones with a cabinet below."

"Have you seen any of those types of tea carts lately," asked Reginald.

"What did you say your name was, sir."

"I'm Reginald North. I guess you don't know if there were any tea carts available for my friend's requirements."

The auction clerk paused, "We did have a client who was going to let us have her tea cart. The cart was an object of art, probably too expensive for your friend."

"My friend's budget is very high? Do you know the appraisal price?"

He heard the clerk pause.

"One million, sir."

Reginald almost fell out of his chair.

"They might be interested. Do you have a picture of the tea cart?"

"No, Mr. North. We don't keep the pictures if the client changes their mind about posting a potential item for sale."

"My friend will be unhappy with no picture. Maybe a description would work. You never know, your client might want to make a sale. Wouldn't you get a good commission?"

The auction clerk licked his lips. He would have to go through his boss.

"I saw the picture and read the description. I think I can divulge those facts. Let me see. I don't recall the exact dimensions. The wood was rosewood or something close. The knobs were elephant ivory and gold. The picture didn't do them justice. Then the inside tray was the same ivory set in gold."

Reginald was typing on his computer the clerk's exact words. He stopped.

"Tell me about the tray."

The auction clerk reiterated the ivory and gold.

"No, no, how did the tray work?"

The auction clerk looked at his other telemarketing agent for their website. The other agent shook her head.

"Mr. North, there was this priceless tray and that is all I can remember."

Reginald knew he wouldn't get any more information from the young man.

Someone in the office stopped the flow of conversation.

"Bad spirits."

"Beg your pardon, Mr. North. Was there another question or some other item on our website that you might be interested in?"

There was a long pause.

"Do you play basketball?"

"No, Mr. North and there aren't any basketballs on our website."

Click. The line went dead to the auction clerk.

The telemarketing person next to the auction clerk leaned over and whispered.

"George, you need to tell the boss about this call. Ms. Kendrell is a very good client of ours. This nut-case might be trying to find the woman or her tea cart."

George left his desk and knocked on his boss's door. After half an hour, George came back.

"Well?"

"The boss said to not take any more calls from Mr. Reginald North."

The two auction clerks wrote the name in their books of creepy characters, get the boss immediately.

Meanwhile, Reginald sat in his office reading his notes.

"The cart that I saw was new. The cart was switched. Ms. Kendrell hid the old and very pricey antique cart from us. The question is why?"

He recognized the tea cart played a role in the missing jewels case. He wondered where the cart was located.

"The woman went to Rome. She took the cart with her."

Reginald looked at the price of a ticket to Rome and winced. Only her lawyer knew the woman's new address. He didn't have any leverage with his old insurance office nor the police.

The auction house manager contacted Horatio Golden about the phone call from Mr. North.

Horatio called Fiona as a courtesy to alert her to the current happenings with the insurance firm. She was informed that the Tiff Sander Jewelers Insurance Company retired Mr. North a few weeks ago.

Fiona thanked her lawyer for the information and told him Mr. North was a dog not wanting to give up its bone.

36 Mysterious Disappearance

Jarret flipped the security camera
off on the wall next to the door of the
cottage. He was off to his doctor's
appointment and would be gone for two
hours.

Fiona was busy reading a book. She
would wait until his return. Then they would
sit on the outside patio and eat the calzones
he would bring back from the bakery.

She heard the knock on the door and
was surprised to see the visitor. He carried a
white scarf in his hands. The man talked
with her over an hour about a wooden
antique tea cart.

She explained the tea cart was placed
in her California garage due to a wheel
problem. For all, she knew, the cart could
still be at the Los Angeles home. The man
yelled at the old woman that he didn't
believe her. Fiona sat serenely in her chair.
He tossed the scarf in her lap and left.

Fiona put the scarf around her neck
and fell asleep.

When Jarret returned, Fiona was
nowhere in sight. He contacted Danielle to
help look for his friend. Danielle walked the
beach and checked the basement. Jarret

researched the garage and walked the neighborhood. Both called the list of taxi and car services on the wall. No service picked her up.

Danielle contacted Craig.

He answered and she explained the disappearance.

"Sandra should be arriving in London. She is scheduled to land in Rome later this evening."

"I've left her phone messages."

"Have you checked to see if Demonte returned to the area?"

Danielle thought Demonte taking Fiona for a ride was a long shot.

"Demonte only likes to hurt Sandra. I probably should have shot him the last time he was here. He is an imbecile, but Fiona is his piggy bank. However, I'll contact his wife to get his location and phone number. She may or may not give me any information."

Danielle learned Demonte should have landed in Rome earlier in the day. She tried his phone number and there was no answer. Jarret contacted the police.

The police searched the home and told the two alarmed people they should go to the police station where they could fill out a missing person's report. Old people were known to walk away from their homes and were later found.

Danielle knew Fiona was not strong enough to walk very far. They left the cottage and drove to the police station in Danielle's car.

When they returned, they found Fiona sitting on a patio chair with her hat on wearing a white scarf. The security system seemed to have been turned on by her or someone else. Danielle would check the cameras but first, there was Fiona to deal with.

Jarret sat quietly holding Fiona's hands when Danielle came to help move Fiona back inside the cottage.

"I'm afraid our friend is gone."

Danielle looked at Fiona in alarm. She took the woman's pulse.

"Oh, no. Sandra is on her way. We need to contact the police again."

"Give me a little time with her."

Danielle went inside and tried Sandra's number. She panicked and called Craig back. He heard her tell him the strange return of Fiona.

"I would leave Fiona where she is until the police arrive. We don't know what happened to her. She could have been abducted or hurt by someone."

Danielle was shaken by Fiona's death.

"Oh, I am so unsure about leaving her outside. Why would anyone want to hurt an old woman?"

"There are lots of reasons. She has money and was one of the last persons to see very valuable emeralds."

"This whole scene doesn't make sense. I'll wait for the police."

The police arrived and then the coroner took Fiona away. The security cameras showed that Demonte turned the house alarm back on accidentally when his hand touched the button before he exited the house.

The police wrote down the information from Danielle about Demonte Duran. They quickly found his rental car at a cheap hostel in the city. They took him into the jail for questioning when he resisted their officers.

Danielle and Jarret waited for Sandra's arrival.

Sandra stepped through the cottage door and hugged the two sad faces. When she heard Demonte was somehow involved in Fiona's disappearance, she knew he was in Rome to beg his aunt for more money.

Sandra contacted Fiona's lawyer who would make his flight arrangements to help with the funeral. He contacted Fiona's doctor in Rome to visit the coroner to explain her progressive illness. Horatio hadn't yet delivered the bronze statue to Demonte's wife. He would drop the box off on his way to the airport.

A call came on Sandra's phone. She stepped outside to feel the cool evening air from the ocean.

"Craig, you were right. Fiona is gone."

"I'm sorry. I should fly out immediately."

"No, let's give the police time to figure out what happened, and I'll talk to Demonte. The police probably won't release him tonight."

Craig bristled on the other end of the phone.

"I wish you wouldn't see him."

"I'll make sure there are either jail bars between us or people around. His visit to Fiona may or may not have caused her death. I have this feeling she might have had two visitors while Jarret was gone."

"Why do you think there was someone else there?"

"Danielle told me Fiona was wearing a white scarf when they found her in the patio chair. Jarret never saw the scarf in her

216

wardrobe before. Demonte doesn't do gifts. There was also a yellow pencil on the counter. Fiona hated pencils. She would throw them in the trash."

"Interesting. Who would have been there to visit her?"

"I have an idea."

Craig wasn't sure he wanted to hear her thoughts.

"Fiona was reading a book when Jarret left. She liked those paper bookmarkers. The bookmarker was folded so the white showed, and she made the marker into a star."

"I don't get why this is important?"

"White rabbit game and a north star."

Craig knew about Fiona's rabbit.

"The emerald switch is the white paper and the star is Mr. North's investigation. You are really stretching things. You believe Mr. North was with Fiona today?"

"Yes. Will you contact his insurance firm? I need to know for sure before I say anything to the police."

"I'll call them. They have a night service to handle calls. I can leave a message for Mr. North."

The pizza boy arrived with a couple
of boxes for their late meal. Jarret put the
calzones in the refrigerator earlier.

Craig called Sandra back.

"Mr. North has retired from the
insurance firm. The service didn't have his
home address or phone."

"Interesting. I'll call you tomorrow
after I see Demonte."

Craig was about to object when his
wife disconnected the call. He knew calling
her back wouldn't change her mind.

37 Jail Visit

The guard ushered Demonte into the small room. Sandra sat down as did her ex-boyfriend.

"You have to tell the police I would never hurt my aunt. You know she was the only person I could trust."

Sandra didn't believe his crap.

"What really happened yesterday? I don't want to hear the police version."

"Fiona knew I was coming for my visit. I talked to her on the phone. I drove directly to her cottage. She was waiting for me. The door and security were off. Fiona appeared to be sleeping. I picked her up and put her in the car. I needed to talk with her without Jarret around. My financial needs are none of his business."

"Fiona was alive when you whisked her away?"

"I tell you she was sleeping. Her hand moved and she had gas."

"Where did you take Fiona?"

Demonte looked angry.

"I was going to take her to a restaurant but missed the turn. I was on the road to the second rebuild house. I drove to the house and there were mover trucks. I didn't know you sold the home. No one ever

219

tells me anything. The house on the hill was my investment, too. Now that Fiona is dead, I'll want my money back."

Sandra ignored his lamenting about the property.

"Where did you go after you saw the mover trucks?"

"I thought she looked odd. She was getting old. I imagined her doctor gave her medicine. I didn't want to get into trouble. I drove her to the cottage and put her in the outside patio chair. There was her hat stuffed in the cushion. I put her hat on. Then I went inside to use the bathroom and left."

Sandra rubbed her forehead.

"You kidnapped her and brought her back. Maybe you were playing the white rabbit game. Keep her for a week until she gives you a huge check and then you return her. Only something went wrong with the game."

Demonte's face turned red.

"She was my relative. I have every right to visit with her. No, I wasn't playing the switch game. You can't tell the police about the white rabbit."

"Yes, you do have the right to visit her."

Sandra was still confused.

"She was wearing a white scarf. Did you bring her a present and leave a yellow pencil on the counter?"

Demonte looked at Sandra as if she was daft. He laughed.

"She threw my box of pencils away when I was little. No, I learned my lesson. Scarfs weren't her thing. Emeralds adorned her neck. Anyway, the jewels used to be there. She wouldn't let me touch the emeralds. However, you got to touch them."

Sandra knew Demonte didn't hurt Fiona. Demonte only disliked her. She decided to tell him.

"I think she might have been ill. She was always secretive."

Demonte thought about her words.

"You think I was driving around with a dead woman in my car?"

"Fiona was gifting items to people. Your wife should be getting a bronze from her lawyer."

Demonte brightened.

"Which bronze?"

Sandra was amazed at the change in the man. His greed was showing.

"The two sweet baby deer statue is what she told me."

"Oh, man, she gave my wife an expensive one. I need to call her right away. We can sell the bronze."

Sandra wasn't sure Demonte's wife would relinquish the gift so easily.

"I'll tell the police what I know about your relationship with Fiona. I'll say you thought you were taking her for a ride. You realized she might need her medicine and brought her back home."

Demonte looked at Sandra. He couldn't say thank you.

"I suppose I'll be handling her funeral arrangements and estate."

Sandra bit her lip. He didn't know she was the administrator.

"Horatio is on his way. Mostly the arrangements are all preplanned. Fiona loved a party so her after-party should be an affair. He will be in contact with you when he arrives in Rome. He will probably see you tomorrow."

Sandra left the jail building.

She sat in Danielle's car and called Craig. She explained the information from the interview.

"Are you okay?"

"Yes, I'm adjusting. The lawyer and I will see Fiona's body one last time. I'll call you when I have more information. He'll know what to do about Mr. North's unsupervised visit. Fiona would have told me if she knew he was coming. I believe he is obsessed. If Fiona hadn't died, I would have recommended a restraining order. He has no business reason to visit per her lawyer."

"Be careful. Now that Fiona is out of the picture, he will need to pursue a different tact and place blame on a different person."

Sandra wondered about Mr. North's reasons for visiting Fiona.

"I should tell him about our wedding gift."

Craig almost jumped out of his chair.

"No, no. I don't want him breathing down your neck or mine. Fiona and Mr. Sloan were having tea before the transport company removed her jewelry. He might want to examine the cart. We aren't going to let him touch anything we own. The man will dream up a story about the tea cart."

Sandra thought about Mr. North rubbing his hands over the ivory and gold knobs.

"You're right. I, however, know where the tea cart is stored."

This was the first Craig heard about her knowledge of the location of their wedding present. She only mentioned the tea cart briefly before. He wondered why the tea cart was so important.

"We'll talk. I'm flying to Rome. Sitting around here is driving me nuts."

"I want you to invite Kevin and his
wife to the funeral. Fiona left me a budget."

Craig was grateful.

"I will extend the invitation."

Sandra got out of Danielle's car and
walked to a small bakery. She bought herself
and Fiona a croissant. She ate hers and
crumbled up the other one for the birds.

"We're going to do this funeral and
play, Fiona."

She was sad there was an end to her
friend's life. Now she would get to play the
violin for Fiona's after-party. Sandra
remembered the dream Fiona told her.

"I wonder?"

She drove to the cottage and honked.
Danielle came outside to the short drive.

"Did the jailbird look bad in plain
clothes? I would have loved to see the cops
with all their guns."

"Very bad. His image was slightly
tarnished. I felt safe in the building. Tell
Jarret we are going shopping."

"Really! I'll be right back."

Sandra knew there was a clause in
the will for the administrator to invite guests
to the funeral courtesy of Fiona. Sandra was
given a pricey budget to purchase a black
dress, shoes, and hat for the funeral as was

Danielle. Jarret already kept a tuxedo in his closet. The tuxedo was made ahead of time.

Danielle came back to the car with her bag.

"We're going to the Maxime Fashion Store on Fiona's money. I'm going to invite Kevin Meadow and his wife to the funeral. He works at Craig's hotel in Security. He's already seen your face."

Danielle smiled.

"Do I get to invite my friends?"

"Yes. Fiona wanted fun. We're going to make sure her wishes come true."

The two women went into the elegant store and rode the elevator to the expensive dresses. She grabbed Danielle away from the shoes.

"Later!"

"But I saw the perfect pair and they might be gone."

"Okay, one pair and then we do dresses."

"What about purses," asked Danielle.

"We do the works!"

Daniella's face brightened.

"Thank you, Fiona."

38 Funeral and Violins

The cathedral was packed with guests and some dignitaries. There was no coffin. Her picture and a white marble rabbit urn were on a small table to the side of the alter. The service, organ and choir music were written to her specific requirements. At the end of the service, the guests drove to a large hotel near the ocean where white tents were waiting.

The hotel served buffet style food and drinks for the guests to mingle. The funeral party friends talked and enjoyed the day. The food was lobster and different kinds of pasta dishes. There were small white fondant cakes with a slice of soft pink fruit candy on top.

Bouquets of hundreds of different types of pink roses adorned the area. The tablecloths on round tables were emerald green shiny fabric. There were no paper plates. The hotel rented fine china and crystal for the event. Champagne in silver containers was placed near the refreshment area. Her urn of ashes was safe in one of the limousines hired for the funeral party.

Craig squeezed his wife's hands. She held her violin case and wore an amazing black dress. She wore white pearls with an emerald drop and white pearl earrings. Craig knew Fiona purchased the necklace a week before she died specifically for Sandra to wear. Jarret gave Sandra the box the day after Fiona's death. This was before she went to Demonte's jail room.

"Knock 'em dead."

"Very funny. You've heard me play and didn't fall over."

He watched her join the orchestra that was assembled under a separate tent. Kevin and his wife joined him. They moved to some reserved chairs and sat down to listen. Danielle, her new boyfriend and old friends were there. Candy sat next to Jarret and the lawyer in the second row. Dawn, Kim, and Darcy sat behind them.

Sandra looked over the crowd and saw Demonte with his wife.

"Won't they be surprised that I know how to play nicely with a full orchestra? Nobody is what he calls me; I don't think so!"

She talked to the orchestra conductor and sat down. Her sheet music was at her stand. The other violinists nodded and sat down.

Sandra could see Craig. He waved to her with a thumbs up. The other orchestra

members assembled, and they readied their
instruments.

The conductor lifted his baton and
they began the first series of songs.

Craig proudly watched his wife play
the violin. He hoped Fiona could hear the
sound. The music drifted along the
shoreline. Kevin's wife leaned over and
whispered, "Heavenly."

Craig nodded his head in agreement.
He looked toward the inside beach wall. The
area for the funeral reception was a private
affair. Craig wondered how the man was
able to enter the area. The man was taking
pictures with his cell phone.

Craig leaned over and whispered to
Horatio. Horatio looked at the place where
Craig pointed.

"You stay here. We don't want to
cause Sandra to turn and watch you. She
needs to keep concentrated on her musical
performance. I'm used to talking with Mr.
North. If he's not a gentleman, I'll notify
security. He also knows Fiona would have
objected to his attendance."

Horatio slipped out of his seat and
disappeared. Craig wanted to watch but kept
his face focused on the orchestra.

Ten minutes later, the lawyer retook his seat. He leaned forward and whispered in Craig's ear.

"Mr. North told me he wanted to pay his respects. I told him the cathedral visit was open to the public. However, he was not invited to Fiona's after-party. This was a private affair with armed guards. He left. I asked one of the security people to make sure he exited the hotel."

"Thanks, Horatio."

"No problem. I detest the guy, too. I believe he was at the cottage before she died. I know Fiona probably handled him. I just wish I could have been there."

Craig lightly nodded.

The lovely symphony music ended. Craig waited for Sandra to put her violin away and shake hands with her fellow musicians.

The new band musicians and singers arrived. The round tables were folded away and a dance floor was rolled into place and secured. The band immediately started playing a fast-paced song.

"Shall we dance?"

Craig took Sandra's hand as other people moved to the dance floor.

"I love you."

Sandra was happy.

"I love you, too."

After two hours of dancing, a black limousine was waiting to escort Sandra and Craig back to their hotel.

Jarret already was home at the cottage with Fiona's urn and his memories.

The dance band finally ended with the last song. A green burst of paper streamers was released over the water. There would be no dismal cemetery for Fiona. Eventually, she wanted to be placed in the ocean.

The stragglers left the funeral after-party. The tents and chairs were removed from the hotel. The long side tables and china were put away. The flowers were donated to various churches in the area.

Sandra touched the perfect emerald and pearls on her necklace. The smoothness of the large green stone was surprising. The moonlight caught a green glimmer of light on the wall of the limousine.

Both knew the ending was the best part of the party.

39 Lawyer at Cottage

Horatio met with Sandra and Jarret in the morning after the funeral to discuss Fiona's will.

Fiona gifted the cottage to Jarret before she died. There was a gift fund set up for upkeep on the cottage and living expenses for services he rendered to her during her lifetime. Jarret was excited to own his own place. He put the documents in his pouch to take to his bank.

"I will leave you two to handle the rest of her affairs. I'll be on the patio or in my room. Help yourself to the refrigerator. The neighbors have been stopping by with flowers and cookies. Oh, here is the shopping bag of presents from Fiona for the six women. She liked to call you, *the club*."

Sandra took the bag. She would see the women tomorrow.

The rebuild second house sale was completed and funds were disbursed per the contract. He gave Sandra a copy of the sale and the will. He showed her all the transactions in the way of gifts that were completed. The large donation items were given out a year ago.

Sandra looked at the dates and the amounts.

"She knew about her illness a year ago."

"No, Fiona knew about five years ago there was an end coming to her life. That is when she started making plans for other people's futures. She loved to be the one in charge. You should have seen her at the rose and garden clubs. Fiona was a ball of fire. She made the city beautiful with all the rose plantings. My wife helped her."

Horatio handed her the smaller charity list of gifts completed within the last six months. She saw the Los Angeles house gift to Demonte and the deer bronze gift to Demonte's wife.

There was a knock at the door. Sandra accepted the tray of bars from another neighbor and their business card. She taped the card to the bottom of the tray and came back to the lawyer.

"Here is the sheet of the projected funeral expenses, travel, hotel, limousines, food, tents, orchestra, cathedral service, urn, etc. I have annotated the invoices we have received. We over-projected on some of the costs. I'll keep you apprised of the final tallies."

Sandra looked at the items on the list. She brought the tray of bars over. The lawyer and Sandra ate a few pieces.

He handed her his estimated final bill. She nodded her acceptance.

"The estate won't have much money left."

"There may be a million or more in the estate. We tried to keep a small buffer amount. She told me there were reasons she wanted to give away her money. I didn't ask her to explain. I deal with known facts for my clients."

Horatio handed her the list of items that were gifted to her. Sandra knew about the tea cart and silver tea service.

"I don't understand."

"You are aware there is a storage facility holding your wedding presents?"

"Yes, she told me and mentioned some pieces of furniture very recently."

Now Horatio was surprised.

"I find those facts intriguing. Fiona didn't tell me."

He frowned. Sandra kept her mouth shut. She waited for the lawyer to finish.

"Do you have any questions about the items listed in the storage facility?"

"There's a beautiful diamond necklace and earrings. The note you added says the items might be missing."

The lawyer relaxed.

"Fiona couldn't remember where she put the velvet bag number twenty-one. The newspaper clipping shows what you might be looking for. The necklace might be in the boxes at the facility. There is so much stuff, it might take the transport people for more than a day to unpack and unload.

"She gifted me the items in the storage facility?"

"Yes, here are the documents. The gifts were made before her death."

Sandra knew she and Craig would be leaving Rome soon.

"When can I access the storage facility?"

He handed her another paper.

"She has paid for the transportation of the items to your home or place of residence or another storage facility or wherever you choose."

"I can wait until Craig and I figure out our life in Las Vegas."

"Take all the time you need. However, transport is only available for six months after her death."

"I see."

Sandra knew Fiona wanted her to hurry. The items in the storage facility should be claimed before the police became aware of them. She wanted two days to unload.

The lawyer handed her another envelope with six letters inside.

"What is this?"

"Fiona wanted to surprise the club."

Craig opened the door.

"Hi, sweetheart. Are you ready?"

He walked over to the shelf in the living room. The white rabbit urn was on the shelf.

"I don't get the white rabbit. Well, maybe I do."

The lawyer and Sandra laughed. They both knew the story about the switch.

Craig grabbed three bars.

"These are good. Fiona's neighbors can cook."

Horatio couldn't help but respond.

"They are Italians."

Jarret heard their laughter and joined the crew in the cottage. More bars were eaten.

"I need to leave. Tomorrow I get to talk with Demonte Duran about his gift and any inheritance."

They let the lawyer move towards the door.

"Thank you all for being Fiona's friend. She talked about you whenever I visited."

They wished him good luck explaining the will to Demonte.

Craig took his wife in his arms.

"We need to let Jarret have some space."

The men shook hands and the couple went to the rental car.

"In two days, we will go to London."

"But I thought we were going to stay longer in Rome?"

Craig smiled, "There's a change to our vacation plans. We have a newly opened hotel in London. My company would like me to meet the new manager. Las Vegas wants to renovate the hotel. I'm supposed to look at their interior design. They also want me to see the new security system."

Sandra's eyes lit up.

"No, you can't go into the security room."

She looked far away. Craig knew that look. He saw her do the look-thing in Las Vegas on her first visit.

"You looked pretty in your dress yesterday."

"Funny, that's the same thing Fiona said when she told me about her dream."

"What dream?"

Sandra climbed in the rental car seat.

"I'll tell you if I can see the security room."

Craig groaned.

40 The Six

Sandra was dressing in the bathroom. Craig sat on the counter watching her.

"I'll be taking Kevin and his wife on a tour of the city. I would have liked to stay for your lunch with your club of women."

She finished putting on the sun-gold matching slacks.

He pushed himself off the counter and held her.

"You look like awesome sunshine in this outfit. It must be new."

"Yes, I couldn't resist the color. The women and I should have a nice lunch together. We don't need my husband getting in the way."

Craig looked crestfallen. Sandra stopped.

"I'll save you some of my desserts."

Craig let her go to greet her friends. Sandra reserved a private room for their lunch. There would be sandwiches, salad, water, and pop. Dessert was ice cream and tiny pastries. She wanted to keep the lunch informal and behind closed doors.

Leaving their hotel room, she carried the small shopping bag and the large envelope with her.

Most of the women were assembled. Danielle was the last to enter and closed the door. The women ate their lunch and sat back in their chairs waiting for their leader to take the floor.

"I know we knew this day would come. We weren't ready for Fiona to leave us. She was good. She kept her words regarding helping us with our investment projects. She wanted us to have a better start in life. I know that I and Danielle are grateful for the time we spent here with her."

All the women nodded in agreement. Darcy spoke, "Fiona was the best."

Candy raised her hand.

"What do we do with the emeralds?"

Sandra looked at her heist club, she needed to let them decide.

"We talked about different possibilities. There's been enough time since the robbery. We could try to sell them in the underground or find an investor. Fiona was afraid we might get arrested if we chose this route. The risk is staring us in the face. My life has changed and I'm not sure I want to pick the life in a jail route."

She let the women talk to each other until they quieted down.

Kim asked, "What were some of the other suggestions?"

"We could leave them somewhere for the police to find the emeralds."

Darcy shook her head as did Dawn and Kim. Danielle stayed quiet.

"We thought about a third scenario. This one seems more believable for the police and insurance company."

Danielle knew what Sandra was going to say. They talked about the risk.

"Fiona has given me the tea cart and her silver tea set as a wedding gift. You all knew about the gift. The tea cart is important as a clue to the investigation. The tea cart is empty. I've also been given some furniture, dishes, crystal, pictures, and other stuff. When I return to Las Vegas, I'll be able to see what is inside of the boxes."

Candy spoke, "She hid them in this stuff."

Danielle looked at Candy.

"Of course."

Darcy interjected, "Where are this tea cart and other stuff?"

"Fiona trusted me with the information recently. She asked that I keep the location a secret. The reason for this is

240

that the insurance agent, Mr. North, is still investigating the theft even though he is retired."

Darcy and the others looked ill.

"Do you think this man is dangerous," asked Kim.

"We need to be wary. At the funeral reception, he was bold enough to sneak into our party and took pictures of us."

Kim muttered under her breath, "Shit."

Darcy stood up. "We've learned our lesson about bad boys and creeps. I put Mr. North in both categories. We give him the ice treatment. We don't know anything about Ms. Fiona Kendrell's emeralds. We stick to our original stories."

The other women agreed.

"When I return to Las Vegas with my husband, a transport truck will deliver the boxes to another facility or our home if we can purchase one. We'll ask the transport company to have their people unpack for us. They will find the jewels. The police will be called, and we believe the insurance company will claim them for their loss."

Candy raised her hand, "Won't the police arrest you as a suspicious suspect?"

Dawn said, "Sandra is willing to take the gamble. We know there's little evidence."

She let her words sink in. Danielle handed out the blank pieces of paper and ink pens.

"Ladies, we have option one, two, or three. Write your answer on the paper and Danielle will collect them," commented Sandra.

Darcy stood up again. "I don't need to hide my vote. Number 3 is an excellent plan. My life has changed for the better, too."

Kim and Dawn spoke, "Number 3."

Candy looked at Danielle.

"Honey, you go first."

"I'll go with Number 3."

Danielle nodded, "I'm in agreement." Sandra held up three fingers.

Candy raised her hand. "Can I keep the ink pen? These are really nice ones."

The women snickered and went to the table to get more dessert and liquid refreshments.

Sandra took the wrapped boxes out of the bag and Danielle put the named envelopes next to the appropriately named jewelry box. The women walked over.

Danielle handed each one their gifts. The women sat down and opened them. There were squeals of delight in the room.

Sandra opened her box and saw the white gold watch with diamonds and emeralds. She read Fiona's card.

Once upon a time, there lived an old woman. She was in a stew about what to do. The Six Ladies entered her life. They were part of a club. They made my time on earth fly. I couldn't resist the watches when I saw the emeralds. I must leave you to find your paths alone. My husband always told me-- remember to hold on to your courage, always walk proudly, and remember timing is everything!
Fiona

Darcy waved her letter. Sandra hadn't yet opened hers.

"You should have given us the presents ahead of time and told us what to do."

Sandra let Danielle take the floor.

"Fiona wanted you to choose. She knew you all had brains."

The women laughed and cheered.

Sandra opened her envelope and read the deed. She excitedly exclaimed, "I have a house in Las Vegas!"

The others told her they were given the title to property or land next to their projects.

Danielle's eyes were bright. "I have a small shop in Rome and I'm pregnant."

The women screamed with more delight. They hugged Danielle and congratulated her. They would be godmothers.

"My new boyfriend, Hank, and I weren't prepared. However, he wants a wedding after the baby is born so I can be skinny when my friends return to visit."

Sandra hugged Danielle.

"Congratulations."

The women stayed fifteen more minutes, took their gifts, and left the luncheon. Sandra waited for the restaurant people to take the food away. She wrapped some dessert in her napkin.

"I would call this a very successful luncheon."

The watch was on her wrist when Craig came home. Within a minute, he noticed. She handed him the deed. He saw the address and went to his computer. The house showed sold but the images were still online.

He and Sandra viewed their new home. Craig saw the golf course close by.

"Nice neighborhood and a short distance to work via the freeway. Fiona knows how to pick the good stuff."

"We have an address for our wedding presents."

She would need to coordinate the timing.

"Oh, I forgot, our tickets arrived."

Craig went to his jacket, brought over the tickets, and handed them to her.

She almost burst out crying. Sandra didn't usually cry. Today was too much. Or rather the whole week was an overload of emotion.

"Did I pick the wrong band?"

"No, I love this group from Australia."

"Great. Your lunch went well?"

"Yes, Danielle and her boyfriend are going to have a baby."

Craig knew they were trying. He held her close.

"I'm pleased. You get to be one of those fairy people."

"The word is godmother. I'm pleased for her."

41 London Concert

The limousine dropped them off at the concert back door where they were quickly ushered inside to greet the band. The leader shook Craig's hand.

"Hey, mate it is good to see you again. Thanks for saving our hotel suite in Las Vegas. I don't know how our reservation got mixed up with someone else's. You came to our aid. There are seats reserved for you off the second floor. I don't want you to get blown away by the lower speakers on the main floor."

Craig introduced his wife to the Australian band members. He remembered their names and instruments. The security person ushered them to their seats. The concert hall began to fill with people.

"Fiona and I went to a concert in London a few years ago after I started dating her nephew."

"She told me about the concert."

Sandra looked puzzled.

"When did she tell you about the concert?"

Craig wasn't sure she should know.

"The first time she came to my hotel in Vegas was when she talked about you."

Sandra suddenly realized which picture Fiona showed Craig."

"No, no."

"Oh, yes. The picture was of you at this same Australian band's earlier concert. Your hair was flying as was your cotton blouse and ripped white jeans. You looked like a creature from the free-spirited hippie era. I think there was a tiny braid in your hair. You wore heavy eye makeup. The lashes looked fake. The rest didn't. Oh, there was a fresh daisy in your jean buttonhole."

Sandra remembered her outfit and dancing crazily. The man next to Fiona took the picture. Somehow Fiona as able to get a copy from the young man.

"My top was really low. You remember the fresh daisy?"

"I did like the white top with fringe. There also was your modeling website. The swimsuit did the trick."

"What trick?"

"You were hard to forget."

Sandra pushed her body into his arm.

The leader of the band came out and the noise level increased as most of the people in the concert hall stood up. The music started playing and Sandra excitedly started swinging her body.

Craig's eyebrows lifted. He took a picture of his wife.

"Perfect shot."

"What?"

"I said we'll talk after the show."

Sandra still couldn't hear him. Craig took the earplugs out of his pocket and showed them to her.

Her laughter disappeared with the other concert sounds. The drums were getting louder as he put the earplugs into his ears.

"This is much better."

Craig sat back and watched the show. After an hour and forty-five minutes, his wife took out his earplugs.

"Dance with me."

Craig recognized the crowd noise diminished and the music changed to a very Latin beat. People were dancing below them in the main concert area. He stood up and danced in the aisle with his beautiful wife.

He was having fun at the concert. Sandra hadn't changed much. Fiona added polish to Sandra. Craig realized at that moment that Fiona groomed his wife. Fiona introduced his wife to expensive tastes. She taught Sandra how to dress and handle men. Fiona taught his wife the importance of friendship.

"Fiona knew I would like the makeover."

Sandra said, "What?"

The volume of sound increased. He yelled.

"Nothing, sweetheart."

After the Latin music songs, the lead player nodded in their direction and bowed.

"This is our notification his security man is ready, and our limousine is here to take us to dinner."

The couple left the concert hall.

"Thank you for the memories. I really appreciated the music."

"Tell me we don't have to see another band concert for five years."

"How about three years?"

"Now, there you go again, trying to get your way."

"How about three and a half years?"

Craig squeezed her hand.

"We have a deal."

42 Intruder

Two months after the funeral,
Sandra looked at her calendar and counted.
She was trying to think about the dates.

"I came to visit Craig here. I
wonder?"

She made an appointment to see her
doctor. The night before, she told Craig. He
assumed her appointment was a normal
woman thing.

"Oh, I'm going to work from home
today. Bring us some lunch after your
appointment and we can eat together."

"I will."

In the morning she drove to her
doctor's office. Sandra answered her
doctor's questions.

The doctor listened.

"Let's wait until after the exam and
results of the tests."

Sandra waited in the lobby and was
escorted back into the doctor's office. The
doctor gave her a prescription for some pills.
Sandra went to the pharmacy and then the
deli. She drove home trying not to think.

She pulled into their driveway, hit
the clicker and drove into one of the three-
car bays. Turning the car off, she hit the

button to close the door. Sandra didn't see the man duck under the door.

The sandwiches and prescription bags were grabbed along with her purse. Exiting the car and garage, she walked toward the back door of the house. The backyard was fenced due to the pool.

She had taken steps across the lawn and was a foot from the door. A man told her to stop. Sandra turned and dropped her bags.

"Mr. North, you gave me a scare. How did you get into my yard?"

"You should be more careful."

Sandra felt a chill run down her spine.

"I'm always careful."

"I know exactly how careful you are. Thieves are careful. You've been exceptionally good at helping Fiona with a heist game and the cover-up. I bet those women at her funeral know all about the switch game. You used the tea cart. Fiona lied to me. The original wood tea cart wasn't in the garage."

Sandra wondered why Craig didn't come out to the backyard. He should have seen her drive into the garage. She saw the school-bus yellow pencil in Mr. North's top jacket pocket.

"Fiona."

She told the women to hold on to their courage.

"I apologize. Your presence is a little unsettling. Fiona didn't ship any of her furniture to Rome. The cottage was too small."

"Where is the tea cart, Ms. Connor?"

"I really have no idea."

Mr. North looked in the air and back at Sandra. His eyes were glazed.

"Your watch is a gift from your dearly departed friend, I suppose. She was into jewels."

Sandra looked at the time. Her husband should be wondering where she was. She watched her intruder as he took a revolver out of his pocket and pointed the gun at her ribcage.

"Here I thought you were the brilliant one of your little woman's club. I must be wrong."

Sandra frowned. She remembered what Darcy called Mr. North. He certainly changed into a bad boy.

"You were at Fiona's cottage right before she died. The police might want to question your reasons for being in her home."

Mr. North waved the gun. The woman in front of him wasn't stupid after all.

"Let me rephrase the question. The tea cart was used to make the switch in jewels, and you have a good idea where Ms. Kendrell stored this tea cart. You will get back in your vehicle and take me to the location."

"You call her lost emeralds *jewels*. They were more than jewels."

"All right. The emeralds were switched using the tea cart. All you or Fiona needed to do was slide the two cases. Oh, I see you are surprised that I knew about the tray inside. Now, move!"

Sandra took the keys out of her purse to stall him. Her purse wasn't heavy enough to hurt anyone. She heard police sirens in the distance.

Mr. North relaxed his arm and lowered the gun.

Craig opened the door, grabbed his wife, and pulled her inside. He slammed the door shut and hit the lock.

She was so startled she couldn't talk. He grabbed her arm.

"Move, we're going out the front door and running to our neighbors."

Sandra stumbled, and he caught her.

"Sandra now is not the time to panic. The police are on their way. They will take care of Mr. North."

"Why didn't you say so earlier? Let's move."

They ran out the front door and over the front lawn. They ran down the winding sidewalk three houses down when Craig pulled her into the bushes and down a wood fence to a large gate. He stretched to unlock the gate from the inside.

Sandra went through the door first and Craig followed. He pulled the gate shut.

"We'll wait here for the police to find us."

Sandra caught her breath and heard a noise. She saw the large Rottweiler approach and stop.

"Nice, doggie. You should go to visit my yard. There's a bad guy waiting. You could chew on his suit jacket."

Craig turned and saw the dog. He said, "Don't move and stop talking."

They waited.

Sandra drummed her fingers on the wood wall.

"He looks friendly. His ears are perky and cute."

"Stop talking and stop tapping."

"I'm thinking."

Craig looked at his wife in desperation.

"All right, but I'm pregnant."

Craig looked at her in total disbelief.

"This is not a good time to tell me the results of your doctor's appointment."

Sandra started getting emotional.

"No, don't cry. The dog is watching."

"Oh, shut up. Mr. North made me drop the deli stuff. I bought the two of us some shakes. Mine was vanilla. I bought you chocolate. I don't usually like ice cream. I don't know what came over me."

Craig rubbed his forehead. The day started out perfectly fine and was now in the dumpster. He wondered if there was any recovery.

"I'll buy you one hundred gallons of ice cream."

His wife wasn't buying the bribe.

"You're not listening."

"You just told me you bought us shakes. Shakes are melted ice cream."

"I'm not thirsty or hungry anymore."

The dog moved back to his spot in the shade and laid down.

"I think the dog has been trained," said Sandra.

Craig looked back at the dog. He took a step toward the gate lock.

"We do this slowly. We'll go out the gate and find a better backyard."

They moved slowly and stopped.

"Be ready. We move at the count of three."

"Three's a good number."

Craig knew Sandra wasn't making any sense at all.

"What difference does it make what numbers I use?"

"You're talking too loud."

"Are we nuts to be arguing in broad daylight with a great big black dog watching our every step? We have a situation problem. Somehow, I encounter situation problems whenever I'm with you. Let me correct myself. Danger lurks around."

Sandra stepped in front of Craig and glared. The dog looked up.

"Look, you are the one who picked this yard for the second incident. Mr. North created the first dangerous problem. I'm the one who is fine."

Craig took one last look at the dog. His wife wasn't fine.

"I'm sorry. You are correct. Let's do this escape thing to get out of the dog situation. We'll work together regarding the first situation."

She turned toward the dog, "Stay."

Sandra marched over and opened the gate.

"Well, what are you waiting for? The dog is staying."

He shoved her through the opening and followed. The latch gate closed. There was no sound from the dog. Craig peeked through the fence. The dog was looking at his tennis ball and ignored the closed gate. He started playing with his tennis ball.

"Whew! You really don't like ice cream?"

"No."

They heard shots being fired close to their spot. The dog started barking. Craig pulled her hand and they were behind a large tree. Craig positioned his wife with her back to the tree.

"We made a baby, finally."

Sandra looked happy.

"Maybe, I can get us bigger shakes."

"Absolutely. We need to eat responsibly. I'll help."

Sandra gave him a kiss.

"Do you think the police have caught Mr. North? He looked odd and asked me questions about the location of the tea cart. He kept a yellow pencil in his pocket. I might have overreacted. My approach probably set him off or the information was wrong. I didn't know insurance agents carried guns."

"He's no longer an insurance agent. Mr. North will be charged. You won't be seeing him in the future."

"Good."

They heard someone on the sidewalk calling Mr. Connor's name. Craig peered out from behind the tree to make sure the man wore a uniform. He waited until there were two policemen and their association's security person before he revealed their presence.

The association security person recognized Craig and his wife.

"We caught the man with the gun, Mr. Connor. You can come out now."

Craig and Sandra approached the three men. Craig felt a little embarrassed that he couldn't have done a better job of rescuing his wife.

"She's pregnant."

The association person extended his hand, "Congrats are in order. You did well in protecting your wife."

Sandra rolled her eyes.

"Let's go home sweetheart. I'll drive us back to the deli."

She handed him the car keys she still grasped in her hands.

"We should get a dog."

Craig rolled his eyes.

"You take the dog for walks."

Sandra thought about her reply.

"I'll walk the dog half the time with the baby stroller."

"Deal," responded her husband.

43 Transport Shipment 1

Sandra watched with Craig as the transport person unwrapped the plastic wrap and blanket from the tea cart. The worker rolled the cart around so they could check the outside.

"The wheels look to be in perfect order," said Craig.

"Interesting."

"I finally get to see the big reveal. I wonder if there is anything inside?"

"Very funny, Craig."

The transport person opened the door.

"Ma'am, there seems to be a package."

Craig bent down and took the package out.

"The note is addressed to me?"

Sandra shrugged. She didn't know what was in the present. She could guess by the shape. Craig unwrapped the item.

"The object is a very ornate and old silver coffee pot. The mark on the bottom is there."

Sandra lovingly held the pot.

"This matches the teapot. I can't believe she found this one. The auction house must have helped her. Fiona knew you liked coffee."

Craig examined the inside of the tea cart and accidentally touched the button on the left side. The shelf popped up automatically to their table's height. He examined the ivory and gold inlay. They were the same stuff as the knobs.

"Wow, I'm impressed. How do we make the shelf go down?"

"There's a button on the right side."

He pressed the button.

"I wonder who the genius was that installed this. The metal looks newer."

"Fiona's husband loved to mess with wood."

The workers unpacked the rest of the tea service.

"We'll need to get the pieces cleaned. They've been in storage a little too long."

The workers unpacked the dishes, serving pieces, crystal, and flatware.

The time showed six o'clock in the evening. The boss of the transport told them they would return the next day to unpack the rest of the load.

"Do you mind Mr. and Mrs. Connor if we leave the truck on the road? We'll make sure the doors are locked tight. We can find a motel close and be back at about seven in the morning.

"Let me call my homeowner association people."

Craig left the room.

"This tea cart is the nicest piece of wood that I've ever seen. No wonder Ms. Kendrell insured the shipment."

Craig returned.

"You can leave your truck for one night."

The man showed Craig the line where he should sign for the items unpacked in the house. He left them alone with the first part of their shipment.

Craig walked over and looked at the champagne glasses.

"I count twenty-four of these long stemware glasses."

"There's twenty-four of all the crystal, dishes, and silverware. Fiona and her husband liked to throw parties in their rose garden. We can sell half. I wonder if Danielle would like some of the dishes."

Craig went to the wine refrigerator and pulled out the champagne. He washed two of the glasses. He was about to open the bottle. He looked at his pregnant wife who walked into the kitchen.

"We're celebrating with a thousand-dollar bottle?"

"I felt relief there were no emeralds in the tea cart. However, we should wait for the champagne."

Sandra smiled. She opened the refrigerator and took out an apple juice.

"You can have a glass of wine."

"Right."

Once her husband was settled, she knew now was a good time to talk about the emeralds. She didn't want to spoil her husband's mood.

"Timing is everything."

Craig finished his glass of wine. His wife looked tired.

"Let's go to bed. There will be more stuff tomorrow. I'm glad we put new flooring in the guest bedroom. Older furniture is very heavy. I would hate to move the furniture twice."

"Fiona told me there was a mirror that attaches to the low dresser."

"I like mirrors."

Sandra yawned. She was four months pregnant. Looking in the mirror was getting harder.

44 Transport Shipment 2

The transport people were with Craig getting his signature on the final delivery.

Sandra looked at the bedroom furniture. The other items were downstairs except for the box of photographs and a large box with a beautiful older style ballgown. She could feel Fiona in the room with her.

"I can't find them."

She paced the floor and looked at her phone.

"I'm pregnant and my thinking is a little off balance. Fiona left two clues. I don't see the clue in the boxes that are downstairs nor in this bedroom. I looked through the photographs. There was nothing. I saw the bottom of the chests as they wheeled them inside. The bed poles are too skinny."

She dialed Danielle's number. Danielle answered.

"The wedding presents have arrived. They are beautiful. The dishes are way too many for us. Would you like me to send you some?"

Danielle paused on the other end. Sandra wouldn't have randomly called her to talk about dishes. Something was wrong with the shipment.

"You're sure there are extra dishes?"

"Overwhelming."

Danielle was advised not to travel in her pregnant state.

"I have received dishes already from Hank's family. Why don't I have Candy come for a visit? She might be interested in the dishes. She is really into stuff like dishes and clothes."

Sandra sat on the bed.

"I would love to see her. Thank you."

Sandra's eyes watered. She was the leader and couldn't find the emeralds.

Craig came upstairs and saw his wife. He sat down on the new mattress they purchased. The mattress was in its original plastic wrapping. He knew his wife was struggling with the bedroom furniture. She held the box for the old pictures in her hands.

"I'll put the pictures back in the box. The box will be on the shelf in the closet. We go downstairs and not think about anything important. The arrival of this second delivery has shaken you."

Sandra looked at her husband. He thought her tears were for Fiona. He was right. Fiona entrusted her with a fortune.

"I called Danielle. She is going to send Candy for a visit."

"Good, I like Candy. I'll pick up some ribs and potatoes. Also, some salad stuff in case she doesn't like my barbeque sauce."

Sandra let go of the box of portraits. She didn't touch the furniture. Her husband came back from the closet. He held his hand out to his wife.

She let him lead her out of the bedroom and downstairs. He knew something was wrong.

"Do you want to share your thoughts?"

"I feel lost."

"I'm here."

She looked at her husband and a slight smile curved her lips.

"I need my friend. Candy helped Fiona at the show. They remained close after the show."

Craig nodded. Candy would be good for Sandra now that Danielle was so far away. He needed to encourage Sandra to remain close to her group.

"I found a puppy from a breeder."

Sandra watched as he pulled out a picture of the mother dog with her brood.

"We can visit them?"

"Tomorrow will work for me."

Craig went into the kitchen to cook chicken. He put a magnet on the dog picture and placed the puppy photo on the side of the refrigerator.

Sandra sat thinking about the pictures. She needed to go through the box again. Craig had placed the gown in the closet on a lower shelf.

45 Candy's Visit

Sandra watched as her husband drove out of their driveway. She raced into their master bedroom and opened her violin case. She grabbed the music sheets, her stand, computer, and raced to the bedroom which contained Fiona's furniture.

There were a few hours before Candy would arrive. Sandra started playing the melancholic song with her recorded music. This was Fiona's favorite from the funeral. When the song ended, she took the box of pictures out of the closet. She took out the large box with the preserved seventeenth-century copy of a ballgown. She looked at the bottom of the dress box.

"Box twenty-one contains a full-length green silk ballgown with golden embroidery down the front and bottom. There's gold lace on the bodice. The sleeves have gathered Chantilly lace. Fiona must have worn this dress to the charity ball. The dress is still beautiful. She's trying to help me find the missing diamond necklace. I still don't understand."

One by one she looked at the pictures from the other box and flipped the pictures over one by one. She placed the pictures in reverse date order on top of the new white bedspread. There were no more pictures. The bed was covered.

The violin stood in the corner. She touched the strings.

"Lost and found."

She turned the box over and read the transport label. The pictures box was numbered three.

"Three was the vote selection we all agreed to use at our luncheon."

She picked up her violin and plucked the strings. The drums were playing in her head. Sandra knew she was close. There was something in the room. She looked at the box she threw on the floor. The green foam fell out.

"All the other boxes contained white foam. The dress box has white tissue."

She picked up the green foam, there was an old black and white picture taped to what was the bottom of the foam. Sandra looked at the picture and raced from the room.

She wore rubber gloves from the laundry room. Pushing on the mirror in several spots, nothing happened. Sandra went back to the picture and saw where the mirror opened.

"Maybe the lock is stuck."

She hit the mirror a little harder.

"If I break this mirror, there will be bad luck. To heck with it!"

She whacked the mirror harder. The mirror opened partway.

Sandra pulled the mirror open wider and saw two rows of open places. There were twenty slots. At the bottom was another open space. The black velvet bags were old with the name of a New York City jeweler stamped in gold on the outside.

One of the bags contained a note with her name. The bag was in the twenty-one slot. Sandra opened the bag over the picture-strewn bed. In her hands was the missing diamond necklace that was gifted to her with matching diamond earrings. The small emeralds seemed to wink like stars.

She went back to the bag labeled number twenty in the mirror. Twenty was the largest gemstones in the collection. The bag was opened on the bed. The large emerald and diamond necklace fell out along with the ring and earrings.

Sandra found Fiona's emerald collection. She sat down in the new chair and looked at the black bags in wonder.

"What do I do with the emeralds? We missed our other plan completely."

She waited until she heard a car in the driveway. Sandra went down to meet Candy.

Candy took her suitcase out of the car and saw Sandra when she opened the garage door. Candy knew by the look on Sandra's face that she found the lost treasure.

Her suitcase and purse were dropped in the kitchen. Candy followed Sandra to the bedroom. She saw the mess on the bed.

"Reverse-thinking always works."

Candy walked over to the open mirror and saw the black pouches.

"Oh, my, the originals are in front of me. I never thought they existed."

Sandra steered her over to the bed. Candy was going to pick up the large emerald necklace.

"No, you need gloves. Here, my gloves are in the room."

With ugly and large gloves, Candy picked up the necklace and lifted the emerald to catch the light.

"This color is pure. I can see Fiona wearing this gem to a ball. I don't believe the size. It's monstrous. This should go to a museum."

Sandra showed Candy the ballgown in the box.

"I love silk. This is incredible. When I get married, I'm going to have white silk dresses for everyone. Can I have the dress? We should check the other black bags."

Sandra already checked them one by one.

"Every piece is here and my diamond gift."

Candy looked at the diamond.

"This setting matches your ring."

"Yes, it does. You can have the ballgown."

Candy started flipping the pictures over one by one.

"These pictures show a beautiful story."

She picked up the photo of Fiona's husband displaying the mirror case in an open position.

"He loved her very much. Here are twenty-one years of anniversary presents before he passed away. Fiona told me I would find somebody. She told me that you and I would go to Africa together."

"I know. She told me the same thing," said Sandra.

Candy picked up the pictures and put them in piles on the dresser.

"We need to clean up this mess before your husband comes home."

Sandra and Candy helped rubber band the photos in date order. They placed the foam in the box with the banded piles and put the box in the closet. They closed the dress box.

Candy put the emerald number twenty jewelry pieces inside their velvet bag. The bag was placed in the correct slot. They pushed on the mirror to close the opening.

"The mirror is stuck. Is there a rubber hammer around?"

Sandra put her bag and necklace in her lingerie drawer out of sight. The single photo was put in the bottom of the photo box. She went outside to the garage and came back with a rubber hammer and a towel from the laundry room.

Sandra looked at the mirror doubtfully. She didn't believe Candy could get the mirror back together.

"No, stop, let's think about this a minute."

"Don't tell me you are afraid?" exclaimed Candy.

"The mirror has already been hit heavily on the glass once before."

Candy felt confident.

"Step back, I'm ready!"

Sandra held the towel as Candy whacked at the corner. They looked at the edges of the wood.

"This mirror looks tighter than before. We did a super job."

The violin, music stand, and sheets were put away. Sandra returned her computer to the den.

Both women looked over the room.

"We have the room in order. Let's go talk."

Candy followed Sandra into the kitchen.

"Fiona mentioned I could sell the bedroom furniture if the pieces didn't fit my taste. I think she was giving me another route."

"You definitely are a sunshine girl. White is probably a better color of furniture for the small room."

Sandra looked at Candy.

"We use the white rabbit story."

Candy wasn't understanding.

"We switch the owners of the bedroom furniture. The idea is a perfect solution."

Candy couldn't help but laugh.

"I need to not be here when this next plan unfolds. They would see my face and know I touched the emeralds. What if the next owners decide to keep the emeralds?"

"I show the police the photograph of Fiona's husband. Oh, no, the gloves are in the bedroom."

Candy went to the bedroom and returned the gloves to the laundry room. She almost bumped into Craig.

"Candy, you have arrived. I know Sandra needs some cheering up."

"I'm the perfect solution, then. I hear you make wonderful barbeque sauce. I can hardly wait."

Craig kissed his pregnant wife and was pleased with the difference. She looked happy. He started preparing his sauce and the rack of ribs.

Candy turned the music on the television set and started dancing. Sandra joined her.

Craig saw the green ballgown box on top of the dryer. He knew Sandra gave Candy the silk dress. He figured that was why they were dancing.

He stopped chopping the onions and watched the two women with their hair flying. The two women put their hair ties on their wrists. They danced separate but seemed to keep the same beat. Craig went back into the kitchen.

"I'm a lucky man. Two beautiful hippie-crazy females are at my house."

He went out to the backyard to put the ribs on the grill. He threw the tennis ball and their puppy chased after the object.

46 African Safari

Craig took his wife in his arms.

"I hate that you are leaving us to play with Candy in Africa."

"You have the babysitter check our daughter's temperature if she even gets a sniffle."

"I will. Maria is six and a half months old and she's not so breakable. We'll be great together. I can work from home some of the days you are gone."

Sandra was ready to leave. He kissed his wife goodbye. He grabbed her arm.

"You take care of yourself. Don't get too close to the wild animals."

"I'll be fine. Candy is the one who's a little frightened by elephants. She needs to get over her fears."

The reminder note was on their refrigerator of the time and date the auction people would pick up the bedroom set. They found a buyer who agreed to pay Craig and Sandra's price.

"Make sure the auction people don't dent our walls when they carry the long dresser away. I can't believe the Auction house took six months to find a buyer. We should have put the bedroom set up for sale sooner."

"You were the one dragging your feet. Once the baby was born, you saw a nice white bedroom set. You liked the smaller size. Besides, I think our guests were afraid to sleep in the room. Fiona's ghost was probably the reason. Even Candy preferred the den when she visited."

"I think you are right. There were spirits in the room. Maybe this house is haunted."

Craig pushed her toward the door.

"Stop worrying and get going."

Sandra smiled. Her husband knew she was stalling.

The next two weeks she and Candy were on their African safari. They got to feed the baby elephants, watch the zebras run, and see a few lions. Another day, a herd of giraffes wandered on the edge of their camp.

Sandra talked with Craig on most evenings. The auction house took away the antique bedroom set to their storage facility and Craig deposited the check. The auction house would deliver the set to the new owners in Los Angeles a day before she returned to Las Vegas.

The time flew by and the two women's vacation was coming to an end. The two women sat by the outside fireplace.

Sandra needed to ask the question.

"Do you ever wish we didn't get involved? I feel guilty about involving the club."

"No. The heist idea inspired us. You could call the plan the final piece to our therapy. We needed to go crazy before we could heal. We can now park the heist in our box. You know like you put your high school yearbook, prom corsage, and favorite teddy bear. The heist is a memory. My future looks brighter. The decision to return the emeralds has brought me closure."

Sandra knew Candy was correct.

"While we were here, life slowed down. The safari tour made me think and do a self-analysis."

"Ouch, I hate looking at the inside. Self-analysis is hard and depressing. You need to stop."

Sandra moved the log in the fire with a stick.

"I think I made a mistake. I shouldn't have kept the velvet bag numbered twenty-one and the photograph."

Candy drank her water from the metal cup.

"If Craig finds them, he will know."

"Yes."

"He will forgive you."

"I'm not so sure," commented Sandra.

Candy squeezed Sandra's leg and walked to their tent. Sandra poured her water on the fire and followed.

Sandra crawled under the covers on the cot. She couldn't sleep. The walls were closing in. Darkness was coming. She could feel the storm raging inside and out.

Large raindrops hit the canvas tent. She missed her violin. Sandra tapped on her cot in time with the noise. Thunder rolled across the tent sounding like drums. Lighting lit the tent and sky. The rain increased.

She knew in the morning the rain would stop. There would be one moment when everything would be clean. The air would be pure, and your vision could see for miles and miles. The water would swell in the rivers and feed the plants with nourishment. The elephants would start walking and frolicking in the sun. The trucks would move across the plains to check the herds. Dust would fill the air and cover every nook and cranny. The earth would be dirty again.

"When I see Craig, he is the moment when my world is clean and crystal clear. He's my rain. Without rain, nothing exists."

She thought about death. Finally, she fell asleep.

In the morning, Sandra skipped the food tent and went to see the elephants. The tour guide approached her.

"We missed you at breakfast. Igbo has come to watch you. She's the oldest of the African bush females."

The elephant flicked her large ear flaps.

"She is very old and crinkled. However, she is extremely sociable and stands still every time I approach. Her name means goddess?"

The tour guide, Mr. Patrick, laughed, "Igbo means goddess of fertility. You have read about Africa?"

"I have a friend named Kim who loves to go to the library."

"We have tagged many of Igbo's offspring. The tags are orange. The younger males are sometimes used to push our trucks out of the muck."

Sandra heard the noisy transportation truck arrive. She turned to the tour guide who was about her age.

"Please come back to visit us again. Igbo will miss you. She senses there is something wrong. If things don't work out, you can come to the Mikumi area again. We like people who have a good heart and like animals."

"Thank you, Mr. Patrick."

"I think you can call me Andie. We have become friends."

"Goodbye, Andie, take care of the elephants."

"Always."

He shook her hand. Sandra turned and left the guide.

The women were packed and ready. The large truck honked the horn. The truck driver was anxious to leave because the ride to the airport was seventy-five miles. The women climbed inside. There were some workers also traveling to the city and hitching a ride. The driver was pushing the speed so they would arrive on time. The rain from the night before made large wet ruts in the road.

After twenty-five miles from the camp, the truck hit a large hole which flattened the tire and threw the truck on its side.

There was a cloud of dust and dirt as the truck crunched over. There was no sound. Sandra felt the air suck out of her lungs. She couldn't visibly see and closed her eyes. There were people shouting.

She blinked and her eyes watered. The side mirror was bent and cracked. Her face was bleeding. The light began to dim. She saw the earth was very close. Confusion settled in her brain. Numbness occurred before she passed out.

"I'm dying."

47 African Elephants

Sandra heard Candy's voice and felt her shake her left arm. She couldn't move. The workers gently placed Sandra against a tree. She heard elephants.

The workers and truck driver were rounding up two younger male elephants with special tags on their ears from the bush. The truck driver knew this was the elephant's area. The driver used a standard voice call to alert the elephants to their presence. The workers placed out some water and food.

The two elephants heard and smelled the food. The call aroused their curiosity. The elephants came running. The driver talked to the elephants while his workers strapped the harnesses over their heads and bodies. They strapped the ropes to the truck sides.

Slowly the elephants walked forward pulling the truck over. The other workers used long poles to brace the side of the truck as they righted the frame evenly to the ground. A large block was placed under the flat truck tire. The frame was lowered more.

The elephants were loosened from their ropes and left to freely eat and drink.

One worker watched them while the truck tire was changed.

"Wake up, Sandra, don't you dare pass out again."

Candy dialed Danielle's number.

"She's hurt. You have to do the elephant song."

Danielle said, "Does Craig know?"

"I didn't know if he knew the song. I'll try to wake her again."

Danielle started whistling. Candy put the cell phone to her hurt friend's ear. Sandra heard the song and tried to smile. She blinked and was thrust into reality.

"My arm hurts."

The workers came and carried Sandra to the back seat of the truck. Candy climbed in the backseat next to her. Candy's scarf was used as a sling to hold Sandra's arm.

The driver and workers climbed aboard the truck.

Candy told Danielle she would call her back when they reached the hospital. Sandra looked out the window and saw the orange tags on the elephants.

"Igbo's offspring."

Sandra passed out again.

XXXXXX

Craig was with Kevin in the hotel security room in Las Vegas when the call from Candy came across his cell phone.

"Hi, Candy what's up?"

He listened to her tell him the story about the truck. He looked alarmingly at Kevin.

"Sandra, my wife, she is safe?"

There was a pause on the other end of the line.

Candy blurted. "She was on the right side. I was supposed to sit there but I didn't. I should have sat in the seat. It's all my fault she got hurt. I don't know what we would have done without the elephants."

Craig was going nuts. His wife was hurt. He told her to be careful.

"Candy, where are you?"

"We're at the hospital. Her right arm and wrist are fractured. She has some bruises and a cut on her forehead."

"I need an answer. Is Sandra all right?"

Candy was shaken by the accident.

"Candy, please."

"They cleaned the dust off. The dust was everywhere. Sandra looks better. She gave us quite a scare. The doctor told us she can go tomorrow. I've made our change in flights. We'll be a day late. I've got to go and get her medicine at the pharmacy. She'll need pain medicine and antibiotics."

Craig relaxed back in his seat. For a minute, his heart stopped.

"I'll meet you at the airport tomorrow."

"We saw on the news the emeralds were found inside the bedroom set mirror. Sandra will want to know if the police want to question the previous owners."

Craig frowned. He didn't want Sandra to worry. This was not the place or time.

"I'll talk to her privately when she gets home. Our lawyer has a document we need to sign."

Candy sighed.

Craig wished he could fly to Africa, but he knew to wait would be better. Their daughter needed her father in the evening.

"They've given her some pain medicine. Sandra is sleepy. We had to get two elephants to turn over the truck and the men changed the tire. We made the decision to continue the fifty miles to reach better medical facilities. I know the ride took its toll. The doctor ordered a lot of fluids when we first arrived. She didn't eat breakfast. They were worried about shock."

"I'm sorry I wasn't there to help.
Should you stay a few more days? I can fly
to Tanzania hospital."

Candy was tired.

"No, Sandra wants to come home."

Craig wanted Sandra home where he
could watch her. There was a problem.

"You get some rest. Just get her on
the airplane in the morning."

Candy hung up. Craig looked at
Kevin.

"I've got to make arrangements for
our daughter."

Kevin watched as his boss
disappeared. He shook his head. He heard
the conversation when Craig hit the speaker
button. His wife wasn't going to believe
him. First, the missing emeralds turned up in
a mirror that was in Mr. and Mrs. Connor's
home for a year and now Sandra got hurt in
Africa while on safari.

"It's the male elephants turning the
truck upright that will make my wife start
baking a casserole to take over to the
Connor house. She's going to want to hear
the whole story because Sandra leads a more
exciting life than she does."

48 Breakup

The Connor's lawyer pushed the document the Los Angeles police requested toward Craig and one for Sandra. They read the document and signed it. The lawyer left them alone.

Their daughter was still with the babysitter.

Sandra was afraid something was wrong. When she arrived at the airport, Craig didn't kiss her. He was waiting with a wheelchair attendant. When they returned to their home in the evening, she was quickly put to bed. He didn't sleep with her and this morning his attitude was cool.

Craig brought her some orange juice.

"I was glad the words were perfect on the document."

Sandra frowned, "What do you mean?"

"The part about where we didn't know there was a jewelry compartment in the mirror before the bedroom set arrived. The police assumed we didn't know because they believed the case hadn't been opened for over five years. The mirror was moved from Fiona's home to storage, from storage to our home, from our home to the Auction storage facility, and finally to the new

owners in California. The jewelry
compartment might not ever have been
found except the mover in Los Angeles
dropped the mirror. The police believe the
jolt moved the lock mechanism and finally,
the mirror released."

Sandra looked at her husband. He
looked upset. She kept quiet. He disappeared
and returned with a black velvet bag
numbered twenty-one. He opened the bag.
The diamond necklace and earrings fell out
onto the table. Sandra picked up her jewelry.

"Tell me where this item came from.
We searched for this bag in all the boxes and
the furniture. We didn't find the bag. Notice
the emphasis on the we-part. This jewelry
has put a knot in your plans. Let's try to
unravel the puzzle."

Sandra felt like she was at an
inquisition. Craig's face was slightly red.
She almost died and he was fuming about
the emeralds. Her heart started sinking. She
caught her breath.

"The bag and diamonds are the ones
listed on Fiona's will. They were missing. I
didn't want them to be lost forever."

"You're not answering my
question."

Sandra shook her head. She couldn't
explain.

He jumped out of his chair and paced the floor. He was using hand gestures to express himself.

"Geesh, Sandra, we had over thirty-five million dollars' worth of emeralds and diamonds in the house. Somehow, you aren't surprised. I'm totally dumbfounded. You could have told me."

"No, Fiona asked me not to involve you. She was correct. You're acting crazy."

"What did you expect? Wait a minute, Fiona knew?"

Craig looked more shocked.

"Fiona knew where her original emeralds were located?"

"I don't know."

"You don't know? How could you not know? She talked to you before she died. Okay, okay. I will calm down. How and when did you find the number twenty-one bag?"

Sandra disappeared and brought him the black and white photograph of Fiona's husband with the mirror.

"I found this when Candy was here. The picture was on the foam on the bottom."

Craig looked at the picture for a long time.

"Why didn't you show me this picture?"

"I couldn't."

"You couldn't trust me?"

Sandra didn't answer.

"We need to destroy this picture."

Sandra agreed. Her husband turned his back and looked out the window into the backyard. His arms were crossed in front of him. There was a long silence between them. Sandra felt cold.

"When is our daughter coming home?"

"Tomorrow around one o'clock, maybe two. I'm supposed to call the babysitter."

Sandra stood up and walked into their master bedroom. She took out her dirty clothes from the suitcase and put them in the laundry. Next, she packed clean clothes in the same space. Shutting her suitcase, she looked around the room. A taxi was on its way.

Craig thought Sandra laid down for a nap. He was surprised to see her with her luggage and winter coat.

"I'm leaving. I'll let you know where I am, eventually."

Craig didn't stop her. He was too upset by the breakup.

49 Snowstorm

The airport attendant helped her put her luggage in the taxi.

"Ma'am, I'm sorry all flights have been canceled. This storm is a bad one."

He shut the door to the taxi. Sandra looked at her watch. The time read five-thirty in the afternoon. The sky was dark, the wind was strong, and heavy snow was falling. The visibility was bad. She gave the taxi driver the name of the hotel in Las Vegas.

Sandra literally was trapped in the city she needed to leave. The hurt inside was too much. She wanted time to think. Craig also needed time.

She thought about Africa. Moving there might work. There were moments of absolute calm to the day. The mornings were the best when the sun rose.

Sandra reached for her large bag with her left hand. The small bottle was uncapped. She took some pain pills and a sip from her water bottle.

The taxi driver and bellhop helped her inside the hotel. She went to the front desk for her set of card door keys. They took the elevator to her room and she gave the bellhop a tip. He closed the door for her.

She sat in the hotel chair more depressed than ever. Craig had every right to be mad at her. Her answers were guarded and all wrong. Sandra could believe he let her go. He would fight her about their daughter. Craig wouldn't let Maria go to Africa until she was older. She deserved the loss of everything.

"True love is overrated."

She looked at herself in the mirror. She grabbed her purse and went down to the beauty shop to get her hair washed. There was still sand from the accident. The beauticians were open until eight.

When she returned to her room, she felt better. The drapes were closed. The glass was very cold to the touch. She slipped off her shoes and jacket and laid down under the covers.

"My dreams are lost. I'm glad the other women's dreams have come true."

In the morning, she awoke and switched on the six o'clock news to check on the weather. The airport looked bad.

"Tomorrow should be better."

She went to the bathroom to wash her face and put new makeup on. Her right arm was wrapped with stretchy fabric. She wasn't supposed to get her arm wet. The hair bonnet was too little. She went to the closet and found a plastic bag.

There was a knock at her door. She believed the person was a maid.

Craig stood outside her door wearing the same clothes from the day before. His face showed a stubby growth of beard. He always shaved in the morning.

"You have spies at the High Tower Plaza Hotel?"

He handed her a glass.

"There are security cameras. We can see across the street and we have excellent zoom capability. Kevin called me. He followed procedures."

Sandra thought about his appearance and yesterday's harsh words. The anger resonated. She still felt cold.

"The heat should be turned up."

She brushed a strand of clean hair away from her bandaged head. Sandra was going to shut the door. She heard the music in her head playing. It was Fiona's song. She looked at her husband.

Craig stood silent in the doorway. He wanted her to choose.

There was hesitation between them. She wondered if he heard the music. She remembered Rome by the pool.

"Do I know you?"

Sandra took a sip of her drink.

"Coconut and a touch of pineapple, how nice! I was right. I don't know you. Goodbye."

Suddenly his eyes brightened.

"I suppose a roomful of flowers and very expensive champagne aren't going to work either."

"You are correct."

Now Craig was at a loss. He kept looking at Sandra. He had the morning. She knew he wasn't going away.

"What is the name of the champagne?"

He told her the name and the year.

"How expensive?"

"A thousand dollars a bottle."

Sandra noticed a change in her husband.

"The rain stopped."

Craig didn't know about the rain. There was snow outside.

She was surprised when he pulled his hand forward. Craig held the champagne bottle with two tall glasses.

Sandra put her drink down on the small table by the door, closed her eyes, and said, "I'll think about the champagne."

Craig stepped in the room, threw the bottle and glasses on the hotel bed, and took his wife in his arms.

"To heck with the rain and the snow. I meant what I said before."

Sandra wiped a tear from her eye. This was the moment. Her eyes brightened. She realized Craig would let her go but then he would follow. Her husband would find her and convince her to come home.

"I forgot what you said."

He kissed her long and soft, ensuring he didn't squeeze her right arm. She relaxed.

"I think I'm remembering the words."

Craig decided to help her along.

"I'll go first. I will love you forever and ever no matter how many secrets you have."

Sandra wiped her nose.

"I'll love you forever and ever and promise to be there."

"That's good enough for me."

There was a knock on the door. Craig stepped aside. Sandra saw two carts full of fresh flowers of every color of the rainbow. The bellhops brought the flowers into her room.

Craig pulled his wife back into his arms.

"We were interrupted."

Sandra bit her lip and opened her mouth. The couple fast-forwarded to the good part.

Both knew forgiveness did exist and was a two-way street. Being separated was not what either one wanted. For them, true love did exist. They wanted more nights together, enough to last a lifetime. The couple kissed for a long time.

Craig said, "I heard the violins."

The champagne bottle was forgotten and was warm to the touch when they left the hotel.

50 A Heist Club

A heist club was no longer necessary. The six women's mission was accomplished. They disbanded the club.

Danielle married her boyfriend, Hank, and continued to live in Rome with their little boy. Darcy became a full-time plumber in Las Vegas and remained single as did Kim who lived with cowboys on her ranch in Cody, Wyoming.

Dawn married a jeweler and remained in Phoenix. Candy went to Africa for three years before she found her doctor and part-time safari guide. She moved to Tanzania a month before her wedding.

The Tiff Sander Jewelers insurance company sold the larger emerald and diamond jewelry to a museum. Private individuals and investors bought the rest of the jewelry. The insurance company recovered its thirty-five million-dollar loss plus interest. There were more than enough funds to pay the lawyers. A measly thirty-five thousand dollars went back into Fiona's estate.

The police were not pressured by the insurance company to charge any individuals because there wasn't evidence of who committed the crime. The insurance company worried their agent, Jim Sloan, might have also been suffering vision problems or was involved in a switch. They certainly knew their former employee Mr. North created a massive problem by harassing Ms. Connor.

Mr. North was placed in prison.

The Tiff Sander Jeweler's public relations people created a small notice in the newspaper about the return of the jewels. The Las Vegas newspaper in collusion with the High Tower Plaza Hotel printed a two-page article about the emeralds and Ms. Fiona Kendrell's life.

Jarret cut out the article and placed the story in a scrapbook. The scrapbook was gift-wrapped with his name in Fiona's closet at the cottage. He found the package a week after her funeral. He knew Fiona loved being in the spotlight. He looked at the older clippings of Fiona wearing her jewels. Most of the pictures were of her with a man at some symphony, charity ball, or garden function. There was one picture that held his interest.

The photograph was of Fiona in a silky seventeenth-century style dress with Jim Sloan. He also was in period dress at the high society charity ball. Jim's arm was around Fiona's waist. They were dancing the pavane, a slow dance of many couples moving in procession. He looked at the back of the picture. The ink writing was in Jim's hand. "We had a lovely time, Jim."

Fiona became the talk of the rose and garden clubs in Los Angeles for years after the discovery. Once the rare green emeralds were found in the mirror of her bedroom set, they could imagine her smiling with joy in heaven. She became a celebrity. They began to enhance the mysterious story of her life by claiming she kept secret lovers after her husband's death.

Demonte forgot to pay the insurance policy on the gift he received from Fiona. The five-million-dollar mansion in Los Angeles was destroyed by fire when the Santa Ana winds picked up. They used the thirty-five-thousand-dollar inheritance to upgrade the kitchen in their current home.

Petrissa kept her job because Demonte worked part-time and received unemployment in between. You could say Demonte was the one who lost the most. Nobody paid too much attention to him, including his wife. She never sold the deer statue.

The couple in Los Angeles who purchased the antique bedroom set from the Auction house became distraught when their home was listed on a Los Angeles company's tour bus guide. On the tour, the bus driver enhanced the sound of his microphone. He called their home, *The Green Emerald and Diamond Discovery of the Century*. The bus driver let the tourists out on the road to take pictures. The family who lived in the home hired Horatio Strong as their lawyer to get their home off the tour.

Sandra and Craig stayed in Las Vegas with their daughter, Maria. Sandra found a job with the symphony orchestra. She became the first violinist. Craig remained with the hotel as the manager. The hotel business increased for both hotels when they found Ms. Kendrell stayed in them.

The Connor married couple found something more *priceless* than green emeralds.

51 Tanzania

Craig Connor looked at the full orchestra. He saw the woodwinds, brass, timpani, and percussion sections. Sandra wasn't in the string section today. The large harp was in view. The men and women of the orchestra were dressed in fancy finery appropriate for the occasion. They were waiting for the limousines to arrive.

Craig adjusted his black tie. He and the other men were wearing white long-jacketed tuxedos. The groom wore a white tie. They wore white shirts and cummerbunds. Their black slacks were neatly pressed, and their black shoes were highly polished.

Craig thought about the day before. He and Sandra went to see the elephants. The guide stepped out of their jeep. They were on a section in the reserve where the younger elephants grazed. The man called elephants. The elephants heard the guide and came running making happy shrieks in between snorting sounds. The guide petted the elephants and gave them treats. Craig and Sandra joined the guide. The day was something he would always remember.

The wedding party did practice their steps and movements two days before. The entire wedding was preplanned months in advance. There was enough time for Darcy to lose weight. She was almost as slim as the other women.

When Craig was informed of the name of the first song in the wedding program, he knew the women selected Fiona's favorite, a music piece written by a French composer. He watched the white vehicles come over the rise in the road.

Two limousines pulled to a stop near the cement curb. The bride's feet touched the ground and the solo flute started playing. The bridesmaids moved out of the vehicles one by one. By the time they assembled into formation, the solo clarinet and bassoon entered the song. The women stood together in a line directly twenty-five feet across from the line of men.

The women wore white long flowing dresses. The white silk was lightweight. The bride's bodice was different. Her top of the dress was covered in lace and shiny beading. Their hair was long with pink roses woven within one small braid of hair. The style of their dresses was identical. From a distance, they looked alike.

The women knew when they were to step forward. Craig watched as the line of women began moving toward them. He knew all of them. They waited until the trumpets joined the music and the snare drum grew louder.

Their hair and dresses blew in the light breeze. The dresses glowed in the African sunlight. Their steps were precision at its very best. The women were one combined force. They held their heads high as they walked in their high heels. Their bodies swayed like models in time to the music.

Craig saw a beautiful image in front of him. The women were equals. Each woman was in control of herself and her movement. They oozed confidence and pride. Craig smiled when Sandra looked at him.

Candy winked at Craig. She was wearing Sandra's borrowed diamond and emerald necklace with matching earrings. Candy was the bride on this glorious day.

The women stood in front of the men and waited until the song ended.

Craig looked at his adoring wife who stood in front of him. All Craig could think of was how lucky he was the day he first saw Sandra in person. She taught the women how to walk for the wedding march and so many other important things.

Sandra and Fiona were responsible for an amazing group of women. He finally understood there weren't just six courageous and intelligent women. There were seven members in the club.

At the count of three, with exact timing, the men turned around, the women stepped forward. The bridal party faced the altar of fragrant flowers. Craig took his wife's arm. Danielle stood next to Craig. She nudged him with her arm. He nudged her back. They were both happy Candy was marrying a doctor. There would be a large reception after the ceremony.

There were hundreds of white and pink roses in a circle at the altar. The orchestra was surrounded by more flowers. The bridal party stood on the emerald green carpet. There was a hush of respect over the wedding guests as a man approached in native dress.

Seven African boys moved to their Ngoma drums. The drums were played with their hands. The deep bass sound reverberated in the space with the sharper sound of the smaller drums. After four minutes of drum music, a minute of silence was observed.

The authorized wedding official moved toward the bride. He asked the pretty bride if she was ready.

The bridesmaids and groomsmen took a step backward. The groom moved forward.

Candy looked at her soon-to-be-husband and answered. Her face was beaming. With confidence, she said,

"I'm ready!"

After the ceremony, the wedding party walked to the reception. Candy and her new husband, Matt, took their plate of food to the wedding table.

Sandra was ahead of Craig. He stopped to answer his cell phone. He looked upset by the call. Putting his phone in his pocket, he looked around the area. Craig saw the man with the gun.

Craig dropped his plate and ran toward his wife who bent to sit down. Craig heard the pop sound and crashed into Sandra, carrying her backward. He put his arms around her head to cushion their fall.

Candy and her husband hit the floor. There were four more popping sounds. Candy's husband crawled over.

"We have to get Sandra to the hospital. She is bleeding and will need stitches. A bullet has grazed her head."

Craig looked at his lifeless wife.

He shouted very loudly, "Guard!"

The guard, Craig, and Candy's husband carried her to the security van and raced to the hospital.

Candy and the others in the wedding party stayed at the reception to calm the guests.

52 The Rain

Craig watched his wife look out the window of their home. She turned.

"The rain has stopped."

He knew about her rain theory. Craig stepped out of the kitchen doorway and stood beside her. The rain was a good omen. He believed in special moments.

Craig was told by the doctor that Sandra should slowly remember her life. There were pieces of the heist she recalled. She remembered Fiona and her women's club.

Three weeks passed since Mr. Reginald North tried to murder Sandra. The police didn't know how he escaped, crossed the Atlantic Ocean, managed to get a gun, and showed up at the reception. Candy had placed a notice in the Phoenix newspaper regarding her upcoming wedding.

Mr. North no longer walked this earth. The security detail at the wedding did their job. They made sure the man wouldn't harm another human being.

Craig didn't push or pressure Sandra. She needed calm. Three weeks was a long time.

Yesterday he heard her play the violin. Craig was hopeful she would remember their life and love together.

She turned.

"You love me?"

"I do."

"You truly love me."

This was a good statement to hear. He lightly kissed her.

"I truly love you."

He watched her face as she struggled to remember.

"I play cards."

He laughed.

"Poker is your forte."

"I remember winning a pot."

Craig wondered where Sandra was going with this morning's conversation. She was getting stronger and did eat two-thirds of her pancake at breakfast. The doorbell rang.

The babysitter arrived to take their daughter to her daycare. Craig helped get Maria dressed and out the door. The dog settled down under the kitchen table.

Sandra was still by the window. He rejoined her.

"Do you want to play poker?"

She quickly responded.

"I'll win."

Craig held his breath. Her eyes were sparkly. She lightly kissed him. He took her hands.

"Why waste all that time with the cards? All you have to say is that I won."

Craig slowly kissed his beautiful wife. The place where they shaved her hair would grow back. She responded and kissed him pushing her body close. This kiss he remembered.

He knew the rest of their life was going to be perfect. They both were given another chance.

Craig said, "Welcome home, sweetheart, you won."

Author's List of Books

Green Emeralds and Heist Club

White Boom and the Seagulls

Gold and the Spotted Jaguar

Raiment Red and a Raven

A Wright Series:

Book 1 – Diamonds Blondes and
Poison
Book 2 – Dead On Coordinates
Book 3 – Wild Golden Obsession
Book 4 – No Easy Target
Book 5 – Powerhouse Race
Book 6 – Cross Paths